Star Sails: Four Pack Volume Two

by

I0552079

Sylynt Storme

PUBLISHED BY:
Lemon Tree Publishing
Copyright © 2012 Sylynt Storme
www.SylyntStorme.com

This is a work of fiction. All characters, names, places and events are the product of the author's imagination or used fictitiously.

Editing: Dragonfly Editing

ISBN-13: 9781927623138

Table of Contents

TIN MACHINES

Carvalho was in Engineering. It was a mess. The fires had been put out, but there were smoldering conduits and spilled bio-plasma units all over the place. Three of his men were helping to clean up. It was a skeleton crew. He'd had almost a dozen men before they lost half the crew on their ship, thanks to the Klethren. Engineering had been particularly hard hit. Three, well, four if you included him, were not enough to repair the problems with both the hyper drive, or Slipknot String Drive, and the LUX drive.

The LUX drive needed only small repairs. Thank God for small mercies. But the hyper drive required much more TLC. They needed gluonite like a burn patient needs plasma. And that was one of the least of their problems.

Engineering required full twenty-four hour rotational shifts. With four of them, they'd have to work a minimum of six hours at a time, with a member on standby. That meant they were really working twelve hours shifts. That wasn't going to be a helpful long term solution. Though Scot Free didn't require sleep. Small mercies again. Perhaps they could use him to fill gaps.

"How are you doing, Ensign?" asked Carvalho to a young man with sweat dotting his face like measles.

"Okay sir, there's just a ton of cleanup to do. And Lieutenant Storey says that our hyper drive is definitely unusable."

Carvalho slapped him on the back.

"We're going to have to double down, ensign. These are going to be a challenging few months, maybe longer, until we get our hyper drive back up."

"Yes, sir."

"Where is Lieutenant Storey now?"

"In your office, sir."

Carvalho left Ensign Schulman and headed into his office. Chuck Storey looked up from behind the desk.

"Sir," he says.

Carvalho waved the formality aside.

"What have you found, Chuck?" he asks.

Lieutenant Storey looks back down at the desk and the schematics on there. He tapped his fingers on it and a holographic image appeared between them. It was a 3D image of the hyper drive.

"Massive expulsion of gluonite, Vitor, and as you can see, there's also been massive fusion of the exhaust vents. Even if we were at Star Ship Command we'd need weeks to repair this damage. Those massive energy surges from Orilion hit our hyper drive pretty spot on and damaged it pretty good."

Chuck was pointing at the different areas of the hyper drive where most of the damage was concentrated. Vitor was grim. He had his arms crossed in front of his chest and had his thumb and index finger cradling his chin.

"Have we plugged the leaking gluonite?"

"We have, but it was all but drained before we put a stop to it. We're going to need at least ten kilograms before we can even think of starting to use the hyper drive again."

"We'll have to find some, then," said Carvalho. "I'll make sure Stone knows about this and makes it a priority. If we ever hope to get home then we're going to have to find more gluonite."

"True, but none of the planets we've made contact with have any. Seems this part of space isn't as concentrated with gluonite as the Milky Way is."

"Then I'd like us to start thinking of other ways to rig this drive so that we might get some faster than light speed up and running, even if it's just a tenth of what we had. Understood?"

Storey nodded.

"That's going to be hard, Vitor, we've never tried something like this, and frankly, I'm not sure the engineering will work."

"Well, if it doesn't, at least we have a project to spend the rest of our lives on. You know how far we are from Earth right?"

Storey nodded again.

"It'll take us generations, probably a million generations to get back home. In fact," said Carvalho, "we'll never get home. This ship has a fifty year lifespan, under optimal conditions, and we're not under optimal conditions."

"Thanks for the morale boost." Storey smiled at his friend.

"It puts it in perspective, then. At least we have something to spend the rest of our lives on. Just keep thinking about it. We're in this together Chuck."

"Carvalho to the bridge." It was Stone's voice over the intercom.

"On my way," he replied.

He was on the bridge less than two minutes later.

"Yes, Captain," he said.

Stone was seated in his captain's chair watching the screen as stars seemed to slowly drift on by. If you closed your eyes to everything that was around you, it would seem like you were a pirate adrift at sea hundreds of years ago. Sailing in the black of night on the Earth's vast oceans.

Stone turned to look at him.

"Please take a seat."

Carvalho sat to Stone's left. Suggs was on Stone's right. He too was watching the slow movement of stars across the main viewer. Almost mesmerized.

"How are things in engineering?" asked Stone, looking back at the main viewer.

"Not good, Captain. We have lost hyper drive and it's going to take a few hours to get LUX drive back up to full capacity."

"So that's why we're limping along like a dog with a broken leg."

"I'm afraid so."

"Well, is there any good news?" asked Suggs.

"No, I'm afraid not, Ty. In fact, if you'd like, I have worse news."

"Worse news?" asked Stone, looking at Carvalho incredulously.

"Yes, Captain. We've completely lost hyper drive."

"Well, get it back then."

"Not that easy. You see, we've leaked just about all the gluonite that we have. We need to find at least ten kilos worth and our exhaust vents are fused along with much of the rest of the hyper drive engine. We need to find a lot of raw materials, including gluonite. But there's more."

"More?" asked Suggs.

"Yes, we need a miracle, too. Even if we were at Star Ship Command, they'd likely need a full engineering crew and three or four weeks to fix this mess."

Stone rubbed his forehead.

"So what you're saying is, that we're lost here in space?" asked Stone.

"In a manner of speaking."

"If I might add," said Scot Free from the helm's seat.

"Yes, please," said Stone.

"We're not really lost, Captain. I have calibrated and fed a direct course back to Earth into the computers. It would be more accurate to suggest that we'll never get there, than we are lost."

"Yes, thank you Scot Free, for that very encouraging news," replied Stone.

"In fact," continued Scot Free, "by my calculations it will take us twenty nine million odd years to get back to Earth if we can use LUX at full capacity which is roughly almost ninety percent of the speed of light. In any event I don't think the LUX drive can sustain that for more than a few weeks at a time. Further, this all becomes a moot point because the lifespan of this ship under optimal conditions is fifty years."

"Thank you Scot Free, that's enough for now," said Stone, shaking his head.

Stone turned to Carvalho.

"If you had what you needed to make the repairs, how long would it take you to fix it?"

Carvalho looked away for a moment to contemplate.

"Well, running twenty four shifts like we are now, and barring any other unforeseen incidents, I'd say we could probably have it fixed up inside three months. That would include any additional help I could get from Scot Free, with your permission. It's gonna be tough, Captain, I'm not gonna lie. We're spread threadbare down in Engineering and the crew is tired. Under ideal circumstances Engineering likes a compliment of twelve. So I believe we can do it with what we have in three, but I'm not gonna make any promises."

"Fair enough. Scot Free?" said Stone.

"Aye, Captain."

"Any spare time you have, if you don't mind donating it to Engineering I'd be grateful."

"Of course, Captain."

"One other thing. We're going to zig zag home. What I mean is, I want us to make way to any planet, planetoid or asteroid that shows promise as having gluonite or any of the other raw materials that Carvalho and his team require. This is now the first priority. We must get our hyper drive up and running as fast as we can. Even if that takes us five years, this is what we must do. We have no hope of getting home for a long time, to paraphrase Scot Free, if we don't."

"Aye, Captain," said Scot Free with a quizzical look on his face.

"What is it?" asked Stone.

"I think you understated what I meant by a large factor, Captain. Perhaps I should have been clearer. What I meant is that none of us will make it back to Earth alive. Not even I, for this ship will not survive more than a few years if we can't keep up with maintenance."

"I think we all understood what you meant, Scot Free. Please keep vigilant for any planets that might offer what we need to make the necessary repairs," said Stone.

"Yes, Captain."

"If you'll excuse me," said Carvalho, "I want to get back to engineering to help my team."

Stone nodded and Carvalho left the bridge. He turned to Suggs.

"How do you think everyone is holding up?" he asked.

"We've got a good crew, Captain. They're first class starship personnel and they're doing their best. Besides, you've got the best first officers in the whole of Star Ship Command."

"Truthfully, though?"

"It's tough on them. But we're just a small group now. There is nowhere else we can go. They'll do their best to serve you, Captain, but I know they could use having you around. Seeing you around. A few good words to the different teams will go a long way. Of that I'm certain."

"Good idea, Ty. I'll start making some rounds to talk to them. Scot Free, all eyes peeled."

"Yes, Captain. We aren't due into another solar system for just under an hour. I'll remain vigilant."

"Suggs, you have the bridge. I'm going to start my rounds with Tactical."

"Aye, Captain."

Stone left the bridge to make his way down to Tactical, which wasn't far from Engineering but on a different deck. He took the lift down and entered the main tactical area. No one was around. He tried the adjoining training room and found five men in combat training. They all turned and greeted Stone as he entered.

"Hello, to all of you," said Stone. "How are you doing, Ensign Delaney?"

"Good. Thank you, Captain," he replied.

"I see you lads are training hard," said Stone looking around at his men. "Things have been rough. I know that all of you have lost some colleagues. We've all lost friends and we're very far from home. But I promise you, that we will do our best to get home as soon as we can. I don't have to tell you that we all have to work as a team in order to make headway. And we have to work harder, put in more time. But you all knew that might have been a possibility when you joined.

It isn't easy, and it's not going to get easier for a bit, yet. But we will succeed on our mission. I have not failed a mission yet, and this will not be a blemish on my record, on our record, or that of the Falcon.

Our first priority is to make repairs to our hyper drive so that we can get home as quickly as possible. To do that, we need to find raw materials for Engineering. They might have to rely on our help. I hope you'll all be as happy to help them as I am."

The group nodded in agreement.

"Good. There might still be some bumpy times ahead. We're now space explorers and we're looking for planets, allies and anything else that can help us get home faster. This is our first and our only priority right at the moment."

Stone went around and spoke to each man in person. Offering encouraging words, asking about family back home. The spirits were buoyed. You could see it on their faces. Afterwards he and Jenks went into Jenks' private office. They sat down.

"It's good to see you and your men staying sharp, Tim," said Stone.

"Well, those of us left, Jack; we have to remain razor sharp. This expedition hasn't turned out as peaceful as we all hoped. We haven't yet many allies, so I'm banking on meeting more malevolence out there. Besides which, physical training is important on so many levels. It helps keeps the spirits up."

"Yes, I wanted to ask you about that. How are the men's spirits?"

"They're good. These are tested men. These are guys who were eagerly awaiting a mission like this. They've trained for years, some of them, for the chance to get out here and face whatever troubles await us. But I'm not going to lie. We've lost some good people. And that stings. The further along this goes, the more difficult it'll be to keep morale up."

"True. We have lost some very valuable people. They will not be forgotten. And this is why our first and only priority is to get the hyper drive up and running. As soon as we can get that, the sooner we'll be home."

"I'm glad to hear it."

Jenks' face was the color and look of a granite cliff. He was battle weary and somber. These last several days had taken their toll. On all of them.

"Stone to the bridge."

That was Suggs' voice over the intercom. Stone got up and told Jenks to come with him. Jenks popped his head into the training room and told Lieutenant Harris to take charge of the remaining training session.

They walked onto the bridge and saw Suggs in the middle of the room looking at the viewer. There was a wavy, distorted image of an alien on the screen. He looked human, if he was a he. But he had a head almost as wide as his shoulder, cobwebbed in veins.

Suggs turned to Stone.

"This is High Council Lorak of Rale. He is asking for our help," said Suggs. "I'll let him explain the problem to you, Captain."

Suggs turned back to the viewer.

"High Council Lorak of Rale, may I introduce to you my captain. This is Captain Stone of the Star Ship Falcon."

Suggs moved his arm palm up towards Captain Stone. Stone stepped into the middle of the room.

"Councilor Lorak," said Stone, "I..."

"It is High Council Lorak of Rale," said Rale, cutting off the captain.

"High Council Lorak," tried Stone again. "I..." Again he was cut off.

"Of Rale."

Stone gritted his teeth. What was wrong with the people in this region of space, he thought.

"High Council Lorak of Rale," said Stone, "I am Captain Stone, how may we help you?"

"We have been stuck underground on our planet for four moon circles. Our people are dying as we cannot get enough food or water to live."

"A moon circle is roughly equivalent to one Earth year," interjected Scot Free.

Stone nodded at him.

"The Unknowns have overtaken our planet and driven us underground, where we live like scavengers."

"Who are The Unknowns?" asked Stone.

"They are our labor machines who raised up against us five moon circles ago, now."

"Scot Free," said Stone.

"I'm on it, Captain," said Scot Free.

"So how would you like us to help?" asked Stone.

"We would be most grateful for any supplies you might spare us, and if you might have the technology to defeat The Unkowns, we would be eternally grateful."

The image wavered and shimmered. The audio was clear but the image was not.

"Let me consult with my first officers and we'll get back to you, High Council Lorak of Rale."

"High Council is adequate from here on out," High Council Lorak of Rale said. "Please hurry, Captain. If The Unknowns determine that you are a threat, they will not permit you here, and worse than that, they might attack. I've sent you our coordinates if you wish to visit us, we'll be waiting. Your hopeful servant."

The screen image was cut and the screen went back to space. In the middle of it was the planet Rale. A dry, hot, arid climate with sufficient atmosphere for humans to get by.

"How odd," said Stone, "now he's my humble servant after tutoring me on how to address him."

Suggs smiled.

"Scot Free," he said, "anything on these Unknowns."

Scot Free turned to Suggs.

"I think the proper term for them is 'The Unknowns' sir."

"Yes, thank you for that. Well?"

"Yes sir, I have identification on The Unknowns."

Scot Free tapped into his computer terminal and an image of a robot appeared on screen.

"They are approximately fifteen feet tall and weigh one ton. They are made of a high density duonium alloy covered in what can be best described as tin plating."

"Tin Machines," said Stone.

"That is only very crudely correct, Captain," said Scot Free. "They are highly advanced by your standards, but not by mine."

"No, I meant they reminded me of tin machines, like the robots I've seen from Earth's middle twentieth century that were used by boys for toys. Square heads, rectangular arms and legs. Not very imaginative looking."

"Yes, Captain, you're quite right. They look almost identical to those old robots," said Suggs.

"Carry on, Scot Free," said Stone.

"They are advanced in the sense that they have laser weapons and some sort of shielding capabilities, but of what magnitude I can't determine without first engaging them to use that capability. From what I can tell, Captain, they were likely used for mining, and their lasers have probably been transformed from laser drilling and mining tools into weapons."

"So you're saying they're an artificial intelligence life form then?" asked Suggs.

"In the crudest sense, yes, you could say so. I don't believe they have the capability to reproduce. But they certainly have the capability to fix themselves and manipulate the purpose of their technology. I think in the broadest sense, I'd suggest that their advanced code has become corrupted, perhaps."

"Could we take them out with a pulson torpedo?" asked Jenks.

"No, I don't think one would work. First of all, we'd need to determine their hub and focus our attack on that. Secondly, we'd likely need to send several torpedoes to decimate them. And I have a suspicion that their network hub has been fortified, at the very least."

"Okay," said Stone. "Jenks, Scot Free, you're with me. We're going to stream on down to the coordinates Lorak gave us. Suggs, you have control of the bridge. Get Carvalho working on figuring out their network relay system or hub. We'll be in contact within the hour."

With that, Stone, Scot Free and Jenks left the bridge.

"I'll meet you in Transit, I'm going to get the doctor. Jenks, bring your best man with you."

Jenks and Scot Free left Stone to collect Commander Kelly. Jenks went to pick up Ensign Delaney.

"Doctor," said Stone to Kelly as he entered Med Bay.

Aimee Kelly looked up from her desk. She was studying something on the computer. She smiled at him.

"What brings you down here?" she asked.

"Well, I need you to visit a new planet with me. The planet Rale. We've been invited there by High Council Lorak. They're desperate for our help. It appears that they have been living underground for four years, ever since their robot laborers had an uprising. They're destitute and need our help. I thought you might be able to provide some medical aid. I'm sure that will be needed."

"I thought we were heading straight for home?"

"We were, until Scot Free informed us that without FTL it would take us twenty-nine or so million years to get home. And seeing as how this ship only has a fifty year operating life, I figured we would do well to seek out supplies and resources to make fixing our hyper drive our foremost goal."

"Good choice," said Kelly smiling at him.

"What are you working on, Doctor?" Stone asked.

"I'm trying to determine the best nutrition protocols for the crew based on the least amount of energy input. The cloning printers on this ship were only designed to last a year what with their supplies. But I think if we ration down to basic nutritional wafers we can extend that to perhaps five years. It also depends on the gluonite we get. If we can manage more of that then we can arguably clone much more food. Nevertheless, there comes a point where the original cell lines become depatterned after so many cycles. So we also need to find additional plants and other food matter that can be stored in the food bank for later cloning as needed."

"Thanks for your help, Doctor. That's going to be an important part of our survival. If we stay out here that long."

Kelly nodded.

"Yes, we have many difficulties to overcome if we are ever to make it back home."

Kelly looked tired and worn out, too. Her face was ashen. Stone reached over and patted her on the forearm.

"We will get home. You have my word."

He smiled. He stared intently into her eyes. But behind the mask, the man didn't fully believe they'd get home at all. He was hopeful and optimistic. Hell, he'd even put good money on it, if they still used money. But he wasn't fully convinced. He would die trying, though, if that was what it required.

"How long do you need, doctor?"

"Just a minute. Let me get my med pack and I'll be right with you."

They met the others in Transit.

"Master Chief," said Stone, "materialize us to the coordinates."

"Aye, Captain," said Master Chief O'Reilly.

They found themselves in a large stone cavern. There was crude lighting all around them. The light was a soft dirty yellow. Far away there was the sound of soft rumbling, like a growling lion or hungry belly.

"Welcome, Captain," said High Council Lorak of Rale.

Stone introduced his men and doctor to Lorak.

"I apologize for our lack of luxuries, Captain, for the last three moon circles we have had to keep on the move."

"That's quite all right," said Stone.

"If you'll follow me, I'd like to introduce you to the rest of our leaders."

They followed Lorak down narrow tunnels barely wide enough for two people to walk side by side. They made some turns and entered a larger room where a table and chairs had been hewn out of the rock.

Lorak went around the table and introduced everyone to Captain Stone and his team.

"This is High Council Norak of Rale. He is our Chief of Annihilation. Next to him is High Council Vlodrak of Rale. She is our Chief of Survival. Lastly, I'd like to introduce you to High Council Molrak of Rale. She is our Chief of Life. Please sit."

Lorak gestured to the five empty rock seats around the table. They all took their places.

"How do you think we might be able to help you?" asked Stone.

"We are hopeful that with your vast weaponry you might be able to destroy The Unknowns," said Norak.

Norak opened up what appeared to be a large plastic sheet. It was flexible and clear. As it opened, it lit up and symbols in Rale came to life. Norak tapped onto the sheet and a holographic image appeared in 3D from the sheet.

"This is the terrain of the area around here," Norak said.

In the image you could see the series of tunnels and a dimly flashing blue beacon indicating where they were. The tunnels were quite a maze. Norak tapped onto the sheet again and the image turned around.

"You can see here, Captain," said Norak, pointing to a mountain range, "that the network hub of The Unknowns is buried here in this mountain. It's only buried about two thousand feet from the summit. We are certain that your weapons could easily penetrate and knock out that energy hub of theirs. From what we have determined, if that network hub is destroyed they should all be immobilized. We had developed it that way as a safety protocol, but we were unable to get there and turn it off after the uprising started."

"How is it powered," asked Stone.

"It is powered through solar energy." Norak turned the image around and pointed at panels on the other side of the mountain. "Here are their energy panels. This area is heavily guarded by several dozen of The Unknowns. Regardless, each of The Unknowns is plated with solar converting energy units which can then be fed back through the ground and into the network hub. It is no use trying to destroy the solar panels. They can each individually keep feeding the energy hub with their own solar power."

"Why do you call them The Unknowns? After all, you created them," asked Jenks.

High Council Vlodrak of Rale answered.

"This is because once we lost the battle against their uprising it became unknown to us what they would do. We've since used the term, The Unknowns, and it is a steady reminder of what we are consistently battling against."

"How far away is their network hub?" asked Jenks.

"Twelve leptons away," said Norak.

"That is about four kilometers, Captain," said Scot Free.

Jenks turned to Stone.

"That is well outside the fallout zone of a pulson, Captain. I think just one torpedo should be able to easily knock it out."

"I agree," said Stone.

"We cannot carry on for much longer than this," said High Council Molrak of Rale. "As you can hear the rumbling, The Unknowns are committed to drilling down and finding us, as such, we must keep on the move. Every four sun circles we must move further and drill further to keep ahead of them. As such, we can barely keep our growing rooms open and the amount of food we can grow in that time is miniscule. More and more of our people are dying with every sun circle. I fear that within one moon circle there will no longer be enough of us alive to continue as a species. Furthermore, every time we head out to scrounge for food we lose men and women to The Unknowns. Please help us."

"A sun circle is about a week, Captain," offered Scot Free.

"If you are willing to help us, then we are happy to offer you any resources that you might need from our home," continued Molrak.

"We will help," said Stone. "But how did things get out of hand with your robots?"

"We're not certain," said Lorak. "It all happened so quickly and we weren't able to determine exactly how or what damage occurred. We think that an asteroid that crashed around five moon circles ago, just before the uprising, was the cause. From what we can tell it appears that this asteroid carried with it a virus that was somehow able to replicate in The Unknown's bio metallic circuitry and rewrite parts of their program. None of our engineers were able to infiltrate The Unknowns so that they could overwrite the code."

Stone tapped his c-star badge.

"Suggs?"

"Suggs here, Captain," came the reply.

"On my mark I want you to fire two torpedoes at the coordinates that High Council Lorak will be sending momentarily. Wait for my command. I think we have a quick and easy way to help the Ralens defeat their uprising AIs."

"Understood, Captain."

"High Council Lorak," said Stone, "is there a vantage point from which we might watch the detonation of our torpedoes?"

"There is, Captain. So far we have one exit out of here that The Unknowns have not yet found. It should give us a good view of the mountain. You will, however, need to wear some suits that we can provide you with for protection against the sun. The Unknowns are slowly trying to poison our atmosphere. It has become hotter and the air more acrid over the past moon circle. This is yet another method by which they are trying to destroy us. And they are succeeding. If we can't stop this shortly, they will create a planet that we just won't be able to live in."

"That won't happen," said Stone, "we'll put an end to this despotism within the next few minutes."

"Thank you, Captain," said Vlodrak.

"My Chief Medical Officer, Doctor Aimee Kelly, would be happy to help in any way to tend to your sick and ill if you'd like," said Stone.

"Thank you, Captain. Doctor, if you don't mind, you can follow me. We have several injured who could use your help," said Molrak.

"I'd be happy to," said Kelly, as she got up and followed Molrak out of the room.

"Gentleman," said Norak, "if you'd follow High Council Lorak, Vlodrak and I will show you how to exit for the vantage point you mentioned."

The four of them got up and followed the three Ralens. They donned some fairly tight suits that were fitted with helmets. They then traveled down some tunnels for a few minutes until they came to a set of metal ladders which were embedded into the rock.

"I'm afraid, Captain that it is a long climb. We have not had the luxury of time to build stairs or back braces in case of fatigue."

Stone stared up at the seemingly never ending ladder. It went on for what seemed like miles. Around every fifty feet or so there was a metal landing that jutted out just to the left or right of the ladder. It had railings on it.

"Those are rest landings if you feel tired," said Lorak following Stone's gaze.

"How high do they go?" asked Stone.

"About a thousand feet up to the surface," said Vlodrak.

"One thousand and nine feet," said Scot Free, looking up at the ladder.

"After you, Captain," said Vlodrak.

"Captain," said Scot Free, "I'll go last if you don't mind. Just in case one of you should fall, I'm likely the best choice to catch you."

"Thank you Scot Free, that's very generous," said Stone.

"Not at all," said Scot Free.

And with that, Stone started to climb. He was in good shape, but he had never had to climb a thousand feet of ladder before. Neither had any of his men. But he had to set the example. He figured he could climb a foot per second vertically. So that would only mean one thousand seconds. Or about sixteen minutes. He didn't want to go to fast. In the beginning, he felt his oats and had to keep himself from climbing faster than he wanted to.

Around one quarter of the way there he started to feel it in his glutes and thighs and shoulders. Just a little bit. Just a reminder that he was working. He was using some muscles.

Around half way, he was counting the steps; it was step number five hundred where he stepped off to the side, onto a metal landing. He was breathing hard. He sat down. The landing could hold four people snugly.

Jenks and Ensign Delaney joined him on the landing after just several minutes. Stone looked down. Vlodrak, Norak and Lorak were off on the landing platform fifty feet below them. They seemed unperturbed by the climb. Scot Free was still on the ladder below the Ralens. Just waiting.

"Wow," huffed Jenks, "I'm getting too old for this. I hope it works. I don't want to have to come back down this ladder."

"Me, neither," said Delaney.

"It's good exercise lads," said Stone with a grin. His breath was almost back to normal.

After twenty two minutes, Scot Free told them, they made the last ladder and onto a large platform that could easily hold a dozen people. Lined up on either end of this platform were narrower platforms with six square holes dug into the rock face. Each of these holes held a harness and a carabiner attached to a rope to allow you to rappel down.

"Thank God, for small mercies," said Jenks.

Lorak came up to a small pad in the wall and tapped into it. Above them, a large circular door opened up. It reminded Stone of an old bank vault. It slid away to the right and bright sun shone through. Lorak grabbed two pairs of binoculars and handed one to Stone. They climbed the last twelve ladders and out into the open expanse. Around them was a clumping of rocks, climbable, but twenty or so feet high. It gave this exit a lot of protection from line of sight.

They all climbed out of the tunnel and up to the top of the rocks. They had a great view of a sloping valley across from which was the mountain in question.

Stone put the binoculars to his eyes and surveyed the valley. Sunlight glinted off several of The Unknowns as they patrolled a kilometer away down in the valley.

"They can't look up," said Vlodrak, "we built them as miners and they had no need to look up."

Stone scanned across at the mountain. You couldn't tell there was anything in there. It was very well hidden. He tapped his c-star.

"Suggs?"

"Suggs here, Captain."

"Fire when ready."

"Firing now, Captain."

In a brief second, they saw what looked like a small fireball shoot from the sky and a second later detonate on the side of the mountain. There was a massive explosion and the top third of the mountain erupted in smoke and debris.

It took a moment to clear. The pulson had made its mark. There was no sign of the network hub. Lorak looked down into the valley. The Unknowns buckled and fell to their knees.

"Thank you, Captain, it appears that it has worked. Look!" he shouted.

Stone looked down into the valley. The Unknowns were tumbling onto their knees. One by one. Then just as suddenly they all started to get up again. They started looking upwards at the mountain where their network hub had once been. Then they scanned across towards them.

"I thought you said they couldn't look up?" yelled Stone.

"They couldn't, Captain. Not the way we designed them," said Lorak.

"It appears they've tweaked their own design then," said Jenks.

A laser blast hit a rock next to Stone. Chunks of it broke off and started rolling down the hill.

"We better get back inside," he said.

"Hurry, Captain," said Vlodrak.

They all ran for the gaping maw that led them back into the tunnel. The Unknowns were slowly starting to climb up the hill. Stone looked back as he was the last one to descend. He saw Scot Free change into one of The Unknown and start walking down the hill.

"Scot Free!" yelled Stone. "What are you doing?"

Scot Free ignored his captain and continued his descent into the valley to meet with The Unknowns. Stone thought of using his pulsar on him. But he decided against it. It probably wouldn't work anyway.

"Dammit!" he cursed under his breath.

They rappelled down the thousand feet in a matter of just a few minutes.

"Where's Scot Free?" asked Jenks.

"I don't know. He changed into one of The Unknown and headed down the hill towards them."

"Dammit Jack, I knew we couldn't trust him."

"Hang on now," said Stone, "let's give him the benefit of the doubt. We don't know what he is up to. He could be trying to help us."

"Come on, Jack, you really believe that?"

"I'm willing to give him the benefit of the doubt," said Stone. "He hasn't let us down yet."

"But we also barely know him."

"Gentleman," said Lorak, "we have a few remaining workable satellites. If you like we can try and tap into them and see if we can find out what went wrong."

Stone tapped on his c-star.

"Suggs?"

Nothing.

"Suggs?"

"Suggs... Captain."

He was cutting in and out and the audio was terrible.

"What's happened?" said Stone.

Silence.

"Suggs, what on Earth is going on up there?"

"Yes... appears that... force field erected. We can't... materialize or launch torpedoes... you... stuck for..."

They followed Lorak, Norak and Vlodrak to the same room they had earlier come from. The sheet was still open on the table. It still showed the schematics of the local area. The mountain still stood proud.

Norak sat down and tapped into the sheet on some lit buttons.

"I'm bringing up the satellite images. This could take a moment. If they're still workable."

They all waited several seconds and then a different holographic image appeared before them. This one was wavy and pixelated. Not as sharp and it shuddered and cut in and out as they looked at it.

"I'll try and enhance it, Captain," said Norak.

The image zoomed in to The Unknowns down in the valley. One solitary Unknown was walking towards them.

"I think that might be your man," said Lorak to Captain Stone.

Stone nodded. What the hell are you doing, Scot Free, he said to himself.

They all watched as Scot Free came up amongst The Unknowns. They circled around him in two layers. There were probably two or more dozen around him. Their hands went up and down as did Scot Free's. The images were small and the quality was still bad. You couldn't tell what was going on.

"Suggs," said Stone tapping c-star again.

"Suggs here."

"Report!"

"Well, Captain, I've managed to fix the audio. I've created two layers of audio; the first one seems to get trapped in the force field that The Unknowns have erected while the second one, the one you're listening to passes by relatively intact. However, this force field makes materialization and pulson torpedoes ineffective. I'm working on it, Captain. But you might be stuck down there for a while yet."

"Understood, Ty. As quickly as you can if you don't mind."

"Yes, Captain."

"We're terribly sorry to have gotten you into this mess," said Norak. "We had no idea that The Unknowns had been able to recreate so much of their technology so quickly. We really thought that if we knocked out their network hub they'd fall like the glacial ice we once had."

Stone nodded.

"We've been in worse situations before. We'll get out of this one. And we'll help you with this problem too."

Norak smiled a nervous smile. The kind you might offer a lion before it eats you.

The image of The Unknowns flickered and then cut out. Molak and Kelly entered the room and took their seats. Stone turned to Kelly.

"How did it go?"

"Not well, Jack. I've managed to alleviate much of the physical suffering, but these people are in desperate shape. There is no one here older than fifty three, and they routinely live over one hundred years. Starvation is rampant and with it are all sorts of the diseases of malnutrition. On top of that, living in such close quarters, there is a nasty virus spreading that is fatal. I have, however, managed to eradicate that threat."

"Your doctor has been immensely helpful to us, Captain. We thank her and we thank you for all of your help so far," said Molak.

Stone smiled at her.

"Captain," said Kelly, "I'd really like to offer them a cloner. They desperately need it, if we are to get out of here that is. It'll take them many months to get back on their feet and a cloner will help them rebuild and give them the nutrition they need to get them over this hump," said Kelly.

"But can we spare it?" asked Stone. "You were just earlier telling me how we needed to start rationing things ourselves."

"Yes, Jack, we can spare it. To save a civilization I'd say we can spare it."

"Okay," he said, and left it at that.

Norak kept fiddling and tapping away at his sheet.

"I think the satellite went into the dark side of Rale," he said. "Hopefully another one should be appearing any minute now."

As if hearing him, the image popped back up to light. The quality was just as poor as the other one but you could make out The Unknowns still circling Scot Free. Slowly, as if falling asleep, The Unknowns started falling down, one by one. Some flat on their backs, others flat on their stomachs and others still at awkward angles. Some of them on their sides and on top of others.

Then Scot Free disappeared, and the image flickered and cut out.

"What was that?" asked Jenks.

"I'm not sure," said Vlodrak. "Norak, can you bring it back?"

"I'm trying," said Norak.

Stone tapped c-star.

"Suggs?"

"Suggs here, Captain, I was about to contact you. I have Scot Free here, at least I think it's him though he looks like The Unknown. Wait, no he doesn't he's changed back."

"Scot Free," said Stone.

"Yes, Captain."

"Report, if you will," said Stone.

"Yes, Captain. When I realized that The Unknowns were still connected to one another after the pulson torpedo hit, I thought I might be able to infect them with a virus. Just like what happened with that asteroid. So I changed shape and joined them. They asked where I had come from and I told them that I had just seen the Ralens and I knew where their secret hiding place was. I connected with one of the leaders of The Unknowns so that he could access my information. But what I did instead was deliver a termination virus that quickly spread through all of them. Any moment now, the last of The Unknowns should be self-destructing."

"Well done," said Stone.

"I had full faith in you," said Jenks.

"Thank you commander," said Scot Free.

Before the battle weary Falcon set sail looking for more raw materials and more importantly gluonite, they met with the High Council of Rale one last time.

Stone and his crew left them with a cloner that would help them rebuild their cities and communities. It would take a long time. There were only a few thousand of the Ralens left, but much of their technology had been saved and archived. The information of it at least.

The Ralens gave Stone several edible plant species. High protein, densely packed nutrition that they could clone to help with their own nutrition needs. They also materialized several hundred kilograms of metal alloys that would come in handy to help repair some parts of the ship that had taken damage over the last several days since they had left Earth. It would also help with the repairs of the hyper drive. But without the much needed gluonite, they would still be limping along on sub-light speed. Hoping and praying that the next planet would offer the gluonite they needed.

Captain's log Earth date 2898.283.13.53:

It's been eight days since we left Earth, and yet we have billions of days left to travel if we are ever to get home. The Ralens have proven to be the first true allies we have come across. And once again, the crew of the SS Falcon owes a debt to Lieutenant Scot Free. It was his courage and thoughtful approach that saved the Ralens from The Unknowns, their very own laborers who turned against them.

We have received the gifts of several plants thanks to the Ralens and they have offered us well over three hundred kilograms of metal alloy that will come in handy in helping us to make much needed repairs to the Falcon. Nevertheless, we are far from home and we have yet to find the gluonite we need in order to have any hope of returning to Earth.

And even if we are able to manage that, what awaits us back home, now that we are a day late, with the promise of annihilation if we attempt to enter the Solar System? Star Ship Command promised to shoot anything down that came into the Solar System a week after we left. That week has now passed. But our first, and still foremost, task is to repair the hyper drive. We'll worry about the bridge back home when we cross it.

SYLYNT STORME

BROTHER'S KEEPER

Stone was sitting in his chair on the bridge. He was watching space and time whiz by leisurely. At least, leisurely compared to faster than light flight. They were a day late and quite a few dollars short, to use an ancient expression. He scratched at his chin. He wasn't certain they could get back to Earth, now. At least, not easily. Admiral Vitran had promised to shoot down any ship that came home after that one week window they had been given. It shouldn't have taken them more than a few days to get out and salvage what they could of the SS Pax. Yet, here they were, limping along in the Virgo Cluster because space out here wasn't as friendly as it first appeared to be.

Scot Free was at the helm, scanning for debris, rocks, planets, anything that might offer even a few grams or more of gluonite. Without gluonite they would never travel faster than light. Without the gluonite they would never make it home. Jack Stone saw an image of himself as a skeleton sitting in his captain's chair. A ghost ship, sailing through the vast ocean of black space. Like pirates, forever trapped to sail these stormy seas.

At least they had received some help from the Ralens. No gluonite unfortunately, but they were able to repair the bulk of the damage to the ship, received over these several days. An added bonus was the plant foods that they could now use in their cloners, to bolster both flavor and substance of the rations that Captain Stone had put the crew on.

He decided to see how repairs were doing in engineering.

"Suggs, you've got the bridge, I'm going down to speak with Vitor," said Stone.

"Yes, Captain," replied Suggs.

Stone left the bridge and headed down to engineering. It didn't take him long to get there. The hallways were mostly empty. The ship was turning into a ghost ship. With about half his crew left, things were much quieter. The mood was much more somber and the crew was working double shifts. It wasn't easy on anyone.

Stone entered engineering and found Carvalho by the LUX drive. He put his hand on his shoulder. Carvalho got up from kneeling and turned to face Jack.

"How are things coming along with the supplies from Rale?" asked Jack.

"Well, that's been the best bit of news we've had since we arrived out here in the Virgo Cluster," said Vitor. "The supplies, the alloys, have been most helpful. We'll likely have the LUX drive fixed by the end of the day or early tomorrow. That should give us extra speed. For what it's worth."

Jack looked around; a few engineering crew members were working independently at different stations, making the repairs.

"Well, I'll take any extra speed I can get," said Stone, "though I'd prefer faster than light."

He grinned at Vitor. Vitor smiled back.

"Wouldn't we all," he said. "But we've got to find some gluonite, Jack, if we're going to have any hope of getting back to Earth in our lifetimes."

Jack nodded.

"It's still Scot Free's first and only priority at the moment. I'll get you some if it's the last thing we do."

"Do you have a plan for if we ever get back to Earth?" asked Vitor. "Like, how will we be able to enter the Solar System without getting shot down?"

Jack brushed his head with his palm. He looked down for a moment.

"Yes, I've thought about that," he said. "We'll have to send a buoy ahead of us to let them know we're right behind it."

Vitor nodded.

"That would work," he said, "we'd need to give it several hours lead on us."

"Agreed," said Jack, "I wish these were the kinds of problems we were dealing with at the moment, rather than trying to figure out how to even get back to hyper drive speeds."

"Well, we have the best men and women on the job, Jack. If we can't get it done, I don't think any other team in Space Fleet could."

"I'll let you get back to it," said Jack. "Your section is my priority, our priority, anything you need to make things happen faster or easier, you let me know."

Vitor smiled at him.

"Did I tell you that we need gluonite? If we had gluonite we'd be as good as done."

Jack laughed.

"You might have mentioned it. Seriously though, is that pretty much all you need?"

"It is, Jack. As I said, the alloys and other materials we've received from the Ralens are enough to fix most of the ship's damage. We should also have the LUX drive up to full capacity pretty quick. So other than gluonite, we'll be all set."

Jack nodded.

"Carry on then."

He left engineering and headed over to Med Bay to see Kelly. He walked into Kelly's office. Dr. Aimee Kelly was calibrating some equipment. She looked up when she saw Jack enter.

"Hi, Jack," she said, smiling warmly at him. She put down a medscanner and turned to face him. She was wearing a white lab coat.

"It's quiet in here," he said.

She nodded.

"There's been nothing to do since we left the Ralens. I let Lieutenant Qualls and Ensign Matthews take some time off. I'm just here calibrating some medical equipment. I need something to do with my time."

"So you're not too busy?" asked Jack.

"No, not really."

"Well, it's not really lunch time and it's not really dinner time, but how about we head over to the mess and grab a coffee for a bit, then?" asked Stone.

"Sure, that would be nice," she said.

They left Med Bay and headed down the hall.

"How is your team doing?" asked Stone.

Aimee looked at him and thought for a moment.

"They're doing okay," she said. "I think Janice, Lieutenant Qualls, is off on a date, if I can call it that, with one of Jenks' men."

Stone looked back at her and raised his eyebrows.

"Really?"

"Yes, Ensign Steven Fouse is his name. Apparently, she's quite smitten with him."

Aimee smiled.

"And your other member, uh, Ensign Mattson?" asked Stone.

"Close, it's Ensign Ellen Matthews," corrected Aimee. "She's a dark horse. She's very conscientious, but very quiet. Doesn't share much with anyone, from what I can tell. So I don't know how she's doing to be honest."

Jack nodded his head as they made their way into the lift and towards mess.

"You know you're not only the ship's doctor, but also ship's councilor now, too."

"I know, I always had an interest in psychiatry, but I decided to focus on space medicine because I thought it was more exciting."

"Well, now you can practice both, in a manner of speaking."

"I'm just a country doctor, Jim, I'm not a magician," said Aimee.

Jack laughed.

"Just give me all you've got, that's all I ask," he replied.

They walked into the mess deck. It was quiet. There were only three other souls there.

"I don't know if I ever told you that, but it was that original space program, Star Trek, over nine hundred years ago, that got me interested in space medicine," said Aimee.

"I didn't know you were that old," he teased.

She hit him on the shoulder.

"You know what I mean."

"I do, and I loved that show."

They went up to one of the cloners and ordered. Jack had a coffee and an apple Danish cloned. Aimee had a green tea and lemon cake cloned. They went and sat down at the far end of the mess deck. It wasn't large. But they had a comfortable booth abutting a large porthole. Outside were millions of blinking stars of all sorts of colors, from deep red to vibrant blues.

"I do love how beautiful empty space is," Aimee said to Jack.

"I know," he said, "I look outside and see how many thousands, millions, of stars and planets there are, and yet the empty space is even bigger. We drift slowly towards home on a large ocean, uncountable fathoms deep and wide and long."

He looked into his coffee with a melancholic look on his face.

"You'll get us home," she said touching his forearm.

"I do hope so. If we can only find gluonite."

In the holospace two figures sat on a blanket on top of a hill. Below them, San Francisco Bay spread out. They were enjoying a glass of red simuhol wine. Next to them was a large loaf of French bread. It had been broken in two, the one side smaller than the other. A chunk of bread lay on a plate between them and in a small bowl was a mixture of balsamic vinegar and olive oil.

"Here's to getting us home... soon," said Ensign Steven Fouse.

They clinked their glasses together in front of the big moon that loomed over the Golden Gate Bridge in the middle of the day, like an all knowing eye.

"That would be nice," said Lieutenant Janice Qualls. "I don't know if I should tell you this, you might think I'm a bit weird, but I miss my cat."

She looked at him smiling softly.

"I don't think you're weird at all. I miss my dog."

"What's your dog's name?" she asked.

He lay down on his side on his one elbow and looked at her.

"Her name is Sirius," he said smiling, "she's a chocolate lab."

He looked away, over at the moon. On the bridge cars were buzzing along in a long steady trail, looking like busy ants. It was peak hour traffic and they were on Hawk Hill in the year 2013.

"And your cat's name?" he asked looking back at her.

She giggled.

"I named him Spock," she said, "because I'm a huge science fiction geek and because he looks like Spock from the original Star Trek, if you're familiar with them."

He nodded.

"Who isn't?" he replied.

"And also my Spock, being a cat, has that same aloof and unconcerned attitude that Nimoy portrayed so well in his character."

Steven smiled.

"I love it," he said.

"He's Abyssinian so he has those big ears too."

Janice was smiling thinking of her cat. She missed him, but being here with Steven made up for it. Well, it almost made up for it.

"This is so lovely," she said looking around at the scenery. "I've never been to San Francisco."

"I'm glad you like it," he replied, "I wasn't certain if I should choose 2013 or 1969."

"Why did you choose 2013?" she asked.

"Well, in 1969 we landed on the moon," he said, "but in 2012 we put the first man made vehicle on Mars. It was hard to choose. But I went with Mars, because it was the first time we had landed on another planet. We wouldn't land men and women on Mars for another twenty five years, but in 2013, the Mars Rover, Curiosity, sent back some startling images that seemed to suggest there was once life there. And in any event, I just love San Francisco. We spent many summers here when I was a young boy."

"It is lovely, thank you so much for sharing this with me."

Steven tore off a chunk of bread and dipped in the oil-vinegar mix and pushed it into his mouth. A drop of oil spilled down his chin.

"Let me get that," said Janice.

She took her thumb and wiped it off his lower lip. Then she sucked it off her thumb.

"You should have cloned some bibs," she said.

He smiled.

"Yeah, sorry, I'm a messy eater. Used to drive my mom nuts."

Jack was taking the last bite of his Danish.

"I'm so glad we had the chance to do this," he said to Aimee.

"Me, too. It's important to spend some relaxation time. All work and no play makes Jack a dull boy. Isn't that how it goes?"

Jack smiled.

"Something like that."

"Captain Stone to the bridge," came Suggs' voice over the intercom.

Stone tapped his c-star.

"I'm on my way," he said. "Would you come with me, doctor?"

"Certainly," she said, they both got up, left the mess and headed straight for the bridge.

Jack entered the bridge with Commander Kelly right behind him. He sat down in his chair as Commander Suggs stood up and took the chair to the Captain's right. Kelly took the chair to Jack's left.

On the viewer was a small spaceship in bad shape. It was smoking from its engines and big chunks of it had been blown off. Wires were sparking in the open.

"Is there anyone in there?" asked Stone.

"Sending a query communication, Captain," said Scot Free.

An image of the interior of the small ship flickered onto the main viewer on the SS Falcon's bridge. There was a lot of smoke around and sparking wires. A young man, perhaps eighteen to twenty years of age looked up. His face was dirty and blackened with smoke and oil. He was slumped in his chair. There was a gash on his forehead that was still wet with blood.

"Help... help me... please."

"We'll stream you on board. Hold tight," said Stone.

He turned to Aimee Kelly, the ship's doctor.

"It appears we need you in Med Bay," he said to her.

"Right away, Captain," she said.

She stood up and tapped her c-star badge.

"Commander Kelly to Transit. Please stream me immediately to Med Bay."

"Yes, sir," came the voice of Master Chief O'Reilly in Transit.

Kelly was materialized out of the bridge and right back into Med Bay.

"Master Chief," said Stone, "as soon as you're done with Commander Kelly, stream the young man in that ship off our port bow directly to Med Bay."

"Aye, Captain," said O'Reilly.

"Scot Free, can you determine if there are any other life signs on that ship?" asked Suggs.

"There are no other life signs, sir. At most, that ship might carry four crew but his was the only life sign found."

"Good enough," said Suggs.

"Suggs, you have the bridge again. I'm heading down to Med Bay to speak with the doctor and find out more about our newest guest."

Stone got up and left the bridge the way he had entered only minutes before. He was back in Med Bay just a couple of minutes later. On one of the beds was the young man. He wore a gray uniform that looked partly like it might have been a spacesuit. Across his left chest was alien writing of some sort. Nothing like what they had seen before. From what Stone could tell, he was unconscious.

"How is he?" Stone asked Kelly.

Kelly didn't take her eyes off him.

"He's stable, now that I've got him here in Med Bay. He hasn't suffered the most terrible injuries, but he has a concussion as well as some internal bruising and the gash on his head which looks worse than it is."

"He looks exceptionally human," said Stone, looking down at the young man.

"He is, externally. Internally too, but he has much larger lungs and heart and his brain is quite a bit more advanced. The sulci and gyri are about three times as many as in our brain..."

"The sulky are what?"

"The sulci and gyri. Those are the folds in the brain. The sulci are the valleys and the gyri are the hilltops of these folds. He has three, maybe four times as many folds."

Stone nodded.

"What does that mean?"

"Well, I can't say for certain until I begin to interact with him, but if I were to guess, I'd say he is probably an off the chart genius. At the least."

"That's good news," said Stone, "we could use extra brain power in trying to figure out how we might get home quicker. Perhaps he could give us some help with remodeling the hyper drive so it doesn't rely on something like gluonite, which seems so rare in this part of space."

"First, I'd like to know more about him and where he came from," said Kelly.

The young man's eyes started to flicker. He moaned. His legs and arms twitched.

"I've given him some painkillers," said Kelly.

She was still holding her medscanner over him.

"He's healing remarkably quickly," she said.

He opened his eyes. They shone with an almost piercing, neon green. Intense and penetrating. He opened his mouth and sound came out. An ancient sounding, harsh language that was not kind to the ears. Stone winced. Kelly put her hand on his forearm.

"It's okay," she said, "you're safe now, we rescued you from your damaged space ship. You are in the medical section of our spaceship. I am Doctor Aimee Kelly and this," she said pointing to Stone, "is Captain Jack Stone, of the spaceship Falcon."

He blinked and opened his mouth again. He leaned up on his elbows. He looked intently into Kelly's eyes.

"I am Cable Wrathwon, thank you for rescuing me."

He was talking in English, the Galactic Translator had not had to translate.

"Where am I?" asked Cable.

"I am not entirely sure," said Stone, "we are also far from home. We are not familiar with these parts."

Cable got up and sat on the side of the bed with his legs hanging off. He looked very much like any American youth in their late teens or early twenties.

"Where are you from?" asked Stone.

Cable did not answer him. He jumped off the bed. He was below average height, at around five feet six inches, and slender. He walked up to the main medical computer and looked at it for a moment. He started tapping into it. Stone watched him warily. After some time Cable turned around and spoke to them.

"I see that I am far from home. I was on an exploratory mission, looking for new mineral deposits that we needed for my home planet of Mon'gol. I got sucked into a wormhole which spat me out against some debris which I crashed into. I think that is when you must have found me."

"Is there anyway we can help you get home?" asked Kelly.

Cable shook his head and looked at her for a moment.

"I'm afraid not. I am also not very familiar with this part of space. I fear I am lost."

"What about the wormhole? We can wait for it to reappear," offered Stone.

"That is kind of you, Captain, but that wormhole is not a stable wormhole. It is rather like a..." he thought about an analogy, "thrashing serpent. It will only reappear here randomly, and I do not think it would be prudent to wait. It could take, how you say on Earth, over a million years."

"How do you know we are from Earth?" asked Stone, both surprised and cautious.

Cable looked at Stone with his bright, green eyes, it felt like Cable was searching his very soul.

"Your computer told me, Captain," said Stone.

"I think you should rest," said Kelly, "I have not yet run all the tests I would like to. You suffered quite extensive injuries. I would like to give you a thorough physical."

"That will not be necessary, Doctor, I am feeling very well."

And he did indeed look very well. The gash on his forehead was all but healed. There was just a small scab where the gash once was.

"I am not a child, Doctor," said Cable.

"You look like one to us," said Stone a little unkindly.

Cable looked over at Stone again, his gaze steady and unwavering, Cable held a poker face.

"My people are renowned for their youthful and energetic metabolisms. I am sixty-six of your years."

Stone raised an eyebrow. He didn't look it.

"What I would rather do is take a look around your ship. If I may, with your permission, Captain?" asked Cable.

Stone looked at Kelly.

"If you allow the doctor to show you around, just in case you need some care, I will allow it. And if you can help, I wouldn't mind you taking a look at our hyper drive in engineering and offering your expertise, if you have any to offer."

"That is the least I can do for saving me, Captain. I will make it my ongoing concern as long as you will have me on your ship."

"Well, there is nowhere else we can send you. You will be our guest until we can help you decide where you might like to be left so that your people might find you."

Cable nodded. He took a hold of Kelly's hand.

"Keep me posted, Aimee," Stone said, as the two of them walked out of Med Bay and disappeared.

Jack Stone made his way back up to the bridge. He wanted to talk to Scot Free about their new guest, see if he knew anything about his people or species.

"How did it go?" asked Suggs as Stone entered the bridge.

"Remarkably well. Kelly is now showing him around the ship. He is both very intelligent, as Kelly mentioned, as well as having a remarkable ability to heal himself."

"I hope she's not going to show him too much of the ship. At least not the tactical areas?"

"No, she wouldn't do that. But I did ask them to take a look at engineering to see if he might be able to assist Carvalho in modifying the drive to see if we can't get FTL without having to rely on gluonite," said Stone.

"That's an interesting idea Jack, have you asked Carvalho about it?" asked Suggs.

"No, not yet."

Stone sat down in his chair and looked at the main viewer.

"Scot Free?"

Scot Free swiveled around in his chair and looked at the Captain.

"Keep our scanners out there for any space/time anomalies, especially wormholes. Also, keep a lookout for any Earth-like planets that might shelter life. I want to try and figure out where this guest, Cable Wrathwon as he calls himself, came from."

"Right you are, Captain," said Scot Free turning around back to his station.

Stone frowned and looked at Suggs. Suggs shrugged. Scot Free was sometimes a little odd.

"One other thing, Scot Free. Can you tell me anything about his species or race?"

Scot Free swung around again to face the Captain.

"No sir, I'm afraid not. I have no recollection of him or his type of species at all. They look very similar to you. Though without speaking with him, I can't say for certain."

"Thank you. If anything comes up, please let me know. Immediately."

"Yes, Captain."

Scot Free turned around again to his computer station and started tapping away at the terminal. He hadn't met many species, and the ones he had, or at least his builders had met, they hadn't come across, yet. Somehow that seemed a little strange to him, but he shrugged it off.

Down in the lower decks of the ship, Cable and Kelly entered Engineering. Carvalho got up from his desk to greet them. He shook hands with Cable as they were introduced to each other. Cable had taken some time to clean up and his wound was gone. There was now no trace at all that he had suffered a gash on his forehead.

"Your Captain was hoping I might be able to help you with your hyper drive. He would like to know if it is possible to modify it so that faster than light is possible without gluonite."

Carvalho looked at him.

"I'm not sure how that is possible. Though it would be a big help considering how rare gluonite seems to be around these parts of space."

Cable nodded.

"Yes, rare indeed. Shall we?"

Carvalho showed Cable to the hyper drive and brought up the schematics on a computer screen close by. Cable studied it for a while, shaking his head.

"No, I'm sorry Commander, but the modifications necessary would require practically a complete rebuilding of the whole drive. I'd say it would be much easier to carry on looking for this gluonite that you need. Indeed, rebuilding this drive would require advanced machinery, the likes of which you'd only find at space docks."

Carvalho nodded.

"I'm inclined to agree. This drive was designed solely to use gluonite which, in our instance, is a highly reusable fuel... Until you lose it all."

"I'm sorry I can't be of more assistance," said Cable.

Carvalho smiled.

"Could you show me to some crew quarters, I'd be very interested in seeing where I might be staying for the next little while."

"I can show you to your very own," she said. "We've lost a lot of our colleagues, sadly, and so we have ample room for you now."

He took her by the hand again as they left Engineering.

"What a strange little man," said Carvalho to himself.

Kelly showed Cable to a room in one of the middle decks. They stepped in through the doorway and the door slid closed behind them.

"It's not much, but this is not a luxury ship," said Kelly, "it's a very basic military ship that was meant for short term missions. A week or two, a couple of months, at the most. As such, the quarters, as you can see, are quite basic."

Looking around, Cable noticed the bunk beds against one wall and two tables and chairs stuck against the wall opposite from the door. Here were two smaller rectangular windows to look out through. A small bathroom was at the opposite end from the bunk beds. In the middle of the room were four chairs and a small square table.

"I have endured worse habitats than this," he said.

"If that is all," said Kelly, "I'll let you get comfortable in your room. You probably want to rest. In fact, I recommend that you rest, and I'll come back and check on you just before dinnertime. How does that sound?"

"Not very good," he said, "I will take you as my mate."

Kelly frowned, she looked at him quizzically, not quite sure she heard correctly.

"I beg your pardon?" she said.

Cable looked at her with cool, arrogant resolution.

"You will be my slave, because I have chosen you. We will mate and you will obey my every wish, for you are a lower form of life."

"I don't think so," she said.

Kelly looked at him. He stood about her height, slim in frame and she wasn't very nervous. She turned around to leave. She felt herself glued to the floor. Her legs felt like they were iron rods hammered into the floor. She couldn't move them. She was frozen solid. Her whole body was immobile except for her face.

"It is simple," Cable said, as he turned her around slowly to face him, "you will obey me because you have no choice."

"I will not," she said, fear in her eyes.

Cable looked at her with those piercing green eyes. Her head was filled with a screeching, high pitched sound that sounded like the death wails of millions of people and animals. Kelly started to cry.

"Make it stop, please, make it stop," she begged.

And as quickly as the screeching sound started, it stopped. She breathed a sigh of relief.

"You will do as I say, yes?"

Kelly nodded. She felt sick to her stomach. This alien had incredible powers of telekinesis and telepathy. She felt like a doll controlled by his thoughts. His mean and brutish thoughts.

"Now is not a good time to mate," she said, "my cycle is not ready."

She was feeling humiliated, seeking any opportunity to escape. Cable looked at her carefully. He believed her.

"Fine, you will bring me some food. The best food and drink that you can find on this ship and you will entertain me then with dancing and music. You have ten minutes. Go now, mongrel species."

Cable sat down in a chair and watched her leave. He was arrogant and he was powerful. His species should never have ended the genetic modifications that had made him one of the pinnacles of his species' genetic development. Now that he had escaped, they would pay for their small-mindedness, and he would rule Mon'gol with these curious Earthlings as his playthings. He leaned back in his chair and smiled to himself.

As soon as Kelly turned the corner from Cable's room she looked once behind her and then ran to the lift. She called for the bridge, nervously waiting, as the lift seemed to crawl all the way up. She stepped out of the lift and onto the bridge.

"Captain," she said.

Jack turned to look at her. She looked as white as a sheet.

"What's wrong?" he asked.

She was breathing heavily.

"It's... it's the alien, Cable. He's evil," she said quickly.

"Calm down," he said. "What happened?"

"He has these powers. I showed him to a spare room, some quarters where he could stay until we figure out where he belongs. He told me I was to become his slave. I tried to leave but he froze me..."

"What do you mean, he froze you?"

Both Suggs and Stone were very concerned with the tone of Kelly's voice. She was visibly shaken.

"I don't know, Jack, I just couldn't move. Then all of a sudden the most awful screeching, loud sound that I have ever heard filled my brain. I thought I was going to literally explode. It was excruciating. I begged him to stop and he did. But only after I promised to obey him."

"So how did you escape?" asked Stone.

"I didn't, he sent me to get him food and drink and told me I had to come back within ten minutes and entertain him. I'm scared, Jack. He's evil."

"So he was actually able to control you somehow?" asked Suggs.

Kelly nodded. Her eyes were wet.

"It's okay," said Jack as he put his hand on her shoulder. "Have a seat."

Stone tapped his c-star badge.

"Jenks," he said.

"Jenks here Captain."

They were on a secure channel as was automatically the case when speaking to one crew member at a time.

"Jenks, I want you to head to crew quarters..." he looked at Kelly and she told him the room number. "Crew quarters 6-011. Our alien guest, Cable, is there. Take a couple of men with you. He is to be considered extremely dangerous. I want you to arrest him and put him in the brig under omega security protocols."

"We're on our way."

"Jenks?"

"Yes, Captain."

"I'm serious, utmost precautions, he seems to have telekinetic abilities. Surprise is likely your most potent weapon."

"Understood Captain, I'll report in less than five minutes."

"Scot Free, see if you can't get a lock on Cable's vital signs."

"Yes Captain, I have him. He is still in cabin 6-011."

"Good," said Stone, "hopefully this will all be over in a few minutes. Put it on main viewer."

They all looked at the main viewer as a schematic of the ship came on and drilled down onto Deck 6. A blue dot indicated the alien Cable Wrathwon. Coming down the hall were three green dots, these would be Commander Jenks and his tactical team. Kelly squeezed her hands. She was nervous but had managed to calm down.

"This should all be over very soon," said Suggs as she watched the screen intently.

The three green dots came up to the door of 6-011. They paused for a few seconds. Two men on one side and Jenks on the other. On Deck 6 Jenks nodded to his two men and flicked two fingers towards the door. They placed a small metal looking object against the side of the door and one of them tapped a code onto the screen. The door opened quickly, silently.

The two tactical officers entered quickly, fanning left and right. Jenks came in and fanned slightly left. Their pulsar rifles were pointed right at Cable. He was leaning back on his chair balancing himself on the two back legs. His arms were crossed in front of him.

He laughed at them.

"You're coming with us," said Jenks.

"I am not," he replied.

Jenks moved towards him. He took one step and fell to his knees dropping his rifle and pushing his hands over his ears. He grimaced. The pain and the piercing noise inside his brain were overwhelming.

One of the tactical officers came at Cable fast, but before he could reach within five feet of him, he was thrown against the far wall where the bathroom was, as if caught off guard by a strong gust of wind.

The second tactical officer pointed his rifle and tried to fire. His trigger finger was torn off his hand and he was tossed up at the ceiling, before being thrust violently hard and fast down again, breaking his back on the chair across from Cable, just in front of Jenks.

Jenks' eyes started to ooze blood as did his ears. He couldn't hear anything except the screeching sound that was driving him mad with pain. And then it stopped. Jenks collapsed to the floor, flopping around like a fish. He was breathing hard, gasping for air. His hands still covering his ears.

Cable bent down and tapped Jenks' c-star badge.

"Captain, you are like the annoying gnat on an elephant. I will squash you."

"Jenks," said Stone, "Jenks, come in."

"Jenks is not feeling well, Captain. I suspect he is going to take a sick day. I am now coming for you. And if you value your life, and the lives of your remaining crew, you will ensure that Commander Kelly obeys me from now on. One step out of place from any of you and I will annihilate you all."

Cable cut the transmission. His blue blip on the main viewer faded and disappeared as he exited his cabin and entered the main hallway.

"Where is he?" asked Stone.

"I don't know Captain, he must have masked his signature somehow. I've tried infrared and that isn't working either, he might be able to mask a temperature signal identical to his surroundings."

"Okay," said Stone, "we're going dark."

Suggs went to a cabinet off to the side and brought out pairs of dark vision lenses for them to wear. He also accessed an emergency pulsar safe and pulled out four pulsar rifles. He gave one to Stone, Scot Free, Kelly and kept one for himself.

"Put on your dark lenses," ordered Stone and they all popped them in except for Scot Free.

"Go dark," said Stone.

Scot Free tapped into his terminal and all lights went off. It was almost black except for the very limited and dimmed computer bio lights.

Captain Stone sat down in his chair and tapped into his terminal.

"Falcon computer," said Stone, "Omega lockdown of bridge."

"Authorization," replied the computer.

"Jack Stone Alpha 0377."

"Secondary Authorization," said the computer.

"Tyrell Suggs Beta 0083," said Suggs.

"Omega lockdown of bridge engaged," said the computer.

"Now we wait," said Stone. "It is my belief he will be headed here to try and grab Kelly. Be extra vigilant. Though I'll be surprised if he gets through Omega lockdown."

"I will deal with him if he makes it in," said Scot Free.

Kelly especially, felt relieved for the android's help.

"You are all ordered to shoot to kill. Set your rifles at maximum."

They all did as Stone instructed. They waited in silence. All rifles pointed at the lift doors; the ship was dark, you could barely perceive it against the black backdrop of empty space. If you listened carefully and you were close enough, you could hear them breath. A little quicker than you might expect. Adrenalin and trepidation was coursing through their blood.

Down below, Cable waited at a lift. The door did not open. He willed it to open and it did, but there was no lift there. He brought it up from a few decks below. He stepped inside. The door did not close.

"To the bridge," he said.

"Access denied," replied a computer voice.

He tapped on the control panel to override, but the lift did not move. He used his mental telekinetic powers to force the lift up to the bridge. He arrived a few moments later. He could see the force field protecting the main door. It was a bio-electric multi spectral field with high enough energy to kill on contact.

He tore it open with his mind as if it were a thin cloth. The space was big enough for him to fit into. The lift door still would not open, so he overrode it with his mind and forced it open fully.

As he stepped into the darkened bridge, Kelly involuntarily fired at him, he altered the course of the pulsar and it splashed against the inside of the lift like wet light. The Falcon had been designed to mimic the electrical impulse of pulsar rifles if used within the ship and as such they had no effect on her.

Cable threw Kelly down on the floor and froze her there. As he did this he bent the pulsar rifles in Scot Free, Stone and Sugg's hands in half, tore them out of their grip, and tossed them into a pile against the far wall. Scot Free leapt at him, much faster than any human.

Cable was caught off guard; he didn't realize they had an android on their team. Scot Free threw him against the far wall. Cable crashed and fell to the floor as Scot Free was on him in a split second. But not fast enough. Cable took Scot Free in his mind, bent him over backwards and stood him on his head and spun him like a top.

Cable got up and walked over to Captain Stone. He slapped him across the cheek backhanded. Stone and Suggs were immobilized. They stood still as statues as Scot Free kept spinning at an incredible rate on his head.

"You insolent little man," spat Cable at Stone.

Cable sat down in Stone's chair and tapped into the terminal attached to it. Then he cursed. He thrust his hand into it, destroying it.

"Will someone please give me light, for the love of all the human failings in space."

Cable looked at Stone.

"I will not," said Stone.

Cable looked at Suggs.

"No," he said.

"You little humans. You little arrogant, small and fragile humans," he said. "I would kill you if I didn't want to be entertained first. Lights."

And the lights came on in the bridge, blindingly bright, brighter than normal. Much brighter.

Suggs, Kelly and Stone blinked and squashed their eyes closed tight. The dark vision lenses were able to adjust immediately and act as shades, but the light was still hard on their eyes, brilliantly bright.

"I did not say you could close your eyes," said Cable.

He took his thumb and forefinger and pulled them apart in front of him and as he did, the eyes of the bridge crew opened wide.

"Arrgh," cried out Suggs.

"I know, poor boy," said Cable. "and you, Captain, the menace you are will sit in front of me and gaze at me adoringly."

As much as Stone tried not to, he was forced to sit, cross-legged in front of Cable with his hands cupping his chin, gazing up at him beatifically.

"You will not get away with this," said Stone.

"Tut, tut," said Cable, "I did not give you permission to speak. Zip it."

Stone's mouth was forced closed, and he couldn't open it. However hard he tried, it felt glued shut.

"And you Kelly, will grovel in front of me," he said.

He made Kelly slither along the floor towards him. When she got to his feet he told her to kiss his boots. She didn't want to, but he forced her to. Then he kicked her in the face.

"Kiss the boot that hates you," he said.

She did, because she had no control over herself. He kicked her again.

"Kiss it," he said.

She did. He kicked her again. This happened a few more times. Kelly's mouth started to bleed.

"For God's sake, you're going to kill her," said Suggs.

"The slave must be punished. I told her," he said. "Anyway, enough from you."

And with that, Suggs was unable to speak.

"Dance a little jig for me, won't you," he said to Suggs. "Do something useful with yourself."

And Cable manipulated Suggs into dancing like a puppet. All the while Scot Free kept spinning like a top and Kelly kept kissing Cable's boot and getting kicked in the face and Stone kept looking up at Cable with a cherubic smile on his lips, gazing in adoration.

On the main viewer, a ship appeared out of nowhere. It was about half the size of the Falcon. It caught Cable by surprise.

"No!" he yelled as he stood up and saw it. He walked over to the computer terminal where Scot Free had sat and tried to engage the engines. He was locked out. He was also not powerful enough to telekinetically steer a ship.

Three alien figures dressed in blue spacesuits materialized on the bridge. They held in their hands large circular disks which looked like small metal Frisbees. Cable tried to manipulate them but their suits protected them from his telekinesis.

They pushed a button on their discs and Cable was enveloped in a white light. Immobilized. Stone, Suggs, Kelly and Scot Free regained control over themselves. Stone stood up and brushed himself off.

"Who are you?" he demanded of them.

The alien closest to him spoke.

"Forgive the intrusion. I am Dred, this is Ayrn and that is Edje," said the alien pointing to his colleagues.

"We are from Mon'gol. We are here to intercept the escaped convict Cable Wrathwon, also of Mon'gol."

"Well, you got here just in the nick of time," said Suggs.

Kelly was picking herself up off the floor, visibly and clearly embarrassed. She smoothed her hair and pulled her lab coat straight. She licked at the corner of her mouth where she was bleeding. She gingerly brought the corner of her lab coat sleeve up to staunch the blood.

"We apologize for the intrusion and any incidents the outlaw Cable might have created for you."

"I am Captain Stone and this is Commander Kelly, Commander Suggs and Lieutenant Scot Free of the starship Falcon."

Stone looked at him.

"Do you mind telling us what has been going on? If it wasn't for your arrival I'm not sure we would be here very much longer to speak with you," said Stone.

Cable tried to struggle against his prison but he was unable to move except for the barest of movement.

"Cable and a few of his fellow prisoners staged a prison uprising at one of our secure facilities. He alone managed to escape in a hijacked ship. We caught wind of his escape only an hour after he left, but it appears he has managed to wreck sufficient havoc already. We followed his signature engine trail here."

"What was he in for?" asked Kelly.

Dred looked at her before replying.

"Many crimes, including rape and murder. But his biggest crime was genetic manipulation. You see, he and his father before him had conducted covert genetic experiments on many people. He was a trusted scientist and used his position in order to gain funding. Over one thousand people have had their genes manipulated by Cable and his father before him."

Dred looked over at Cable with a look that almost resembled pity.

"By the time the ethics board, which had been stifled from investigating his research due to political maneuverings, was able to investigate, much of the damage had been done. As you can tell, the manipulation creates extreme intelligence and powers, but it also carries exceptional risks. Violent, arrogant behavior being the most prevalent."

Stone nodded.

"At first the research was aimed at helping uncover cures for disease and disabilities, but the Wrathwon's lust for power soon got the best of them and they created this army of genetically advanced beings, who turned out to be violent criminals attempting to overthrow the state."

"Are there any others who have escaped that we might need to be concerned about?" asked Stone.

"No. He was the only one who escaped. As you can imagine, genetic manipulation has been banned on our planet."

Dred looked at his two colleagues who had Cable securely between them, enclosed in his prison of light. The three of them materialized off the Falcon.

"I am authorized to offer compensation for your difficulties as well as help in Cable Wrathwon's capture. Is there anything you might need that we can help with?" asked Dred.

Stone looked around at his team. Then he thought of Carvalho.

"Well, I'll just put it out there, but if you have gluonite we could sure use some?"

Dred nodded.

"We have gluonite. Follow us to our home planet and we will be sure to help you with any needed repairs and as much gluonite as you might need. Again Captain, on behalf of the people of Mon'gol we apologize for the difficulties Cable has caused."

Stone nodded.

"All for trying to help a stranger out," he said.

Dred smiled at him and then materialized off the Falcon.

WORM TURNS

Captain's log 2898.287.08.00. We are just leaving Mon'gol after a well-deserved rest of four days. The Mon'golins have been gracious hosts and fine friends. They have helped us immensely with much needed gluonite. In addition to that they helped us complete the repairs to the hyper drive engines. We haven't had a chance to test them out yet, but that will be our first order of business once we have left their system.

However, we are five days late already in getting back to Earth. Our approach will have to be dark and quiet. We'll send a buoy out ahead of us once we have reached the galaxy. All going well, we will likely arrive sometime this evening, or perhaps tomorrow morning, at the latest.

I speak for all of us when I say that we will be very happy to be back home on terra firma.

Captain Stone signed off from the log and locked the access to his command terminal. The desk in front of him turned dark and went back to a normal desk. The color was a transparent metallic glass. He looked around the ready room. It was small. His desk, which was also a computer and emergency command center, and his chair. Across from him was a small sofa. That was it. This was a warship after all. It had no unnecessary comforts.

He leaned on his hands for a moment to find some rest and peace. These twelve days had been chaotic. He had never, in his worst nightmares, imagined that deep outer space would be so inhospitable to humans. It was eye opening. He was looking forward to getting home and taking some time off. Perhaps visit the woods back home in Alaska.

He got up from his chair and stood by the window with his hands clasped behind his back. He was looking out at the rocky Martian looking planet of Mon'gol. It was redder than Mars' rusty look. It wasn't all that hot, in fact it erred on the cool side. Much like a constant fall. The Mon'golins had been extremely helpful, but he was not unhappy to be leaving them for a few reasons. Not the least of which was the fact that he had difficulties with the genetically manipulated population that they had locked up on Crime Dock Desamonis. Cable was a living example of the Pandora's box to be opened in the event that genetic manipulation was allowed to develop without oversight. Thankfully, humanity had put an end to all but the most rudimentary genetic manipulation. It had been found unnecessary to manipulate genes and still extend life and the quality of it.

But the Mon'golins, he thought, were in for a long autumn where continued vigilance would be required in order to maintain political and social stability. Many citizens had friends and relatives locked away because they had been genetically manipulated.

Stone watched the planet get smaller and smaller as they made their way out of this system. He watched it until it was the size of a small marble. Then he turned around and walked out of his ready room. Suggs was on the bridge in command. He looked towards his Captain.

"Good to be leaving for home," he said.

Stone nodded.

"Yes it is, Ty. As soon as we've cleared this system and I've confirmed with engineering that our hyper drive is capable, we'll start our FTL flight back home. Perhaps we'll make it home in time for dinner. One can dream," Stone said.

Stone gave a weary smile.

"I believe in the power of dreams," Suggs said.

Stone came over and put his hand on his friend's shoulder.

"Give me a minute. I'm going down to engineering to speak with Carvalho. Let's hope good news abounds."

Suggs nodded.

"I think Vitor will have nothing but good news for you, Captain," replied Suggs.

Stone left the bridge and took the lift down towards engineering. The hallways were still empty, with only the memories of lost men and women who had once walked them. He didn't think much about that. It wasn't helpful and it didn't make it any easier with the task at hand.

He entered engineering. There was only one woman manning the computer banks that controlled the main engines. He peeked into the office and saw Carvalho hunched over his desk looking at computer schematics that the desk was displaying.

"Commander," said Stone.

Carvalho looked up, taken by surprise.

"Captain," he said, walking up from behind his desk.

Stone put his hand up and took the chair opposite the desk from Carvalho. Carvalho sat back down.

"What brings you here, Jack?" asked Carvalho.

"Well, I wanted to get final confirmation from you that our engines are ready to get back into FTL, before I give the bridge the go ahead."

Carvalho looked back down at his schematics and then tapped some touchscreen buttons and the image appeared between them on the vertical. Carvalho pointed to some numbers and graphs.

"She's humming along at near perfect specifications Jack. It's like she was built just yesterday. If this keeps up we'll be in good shape for the ride home."

"Any concerns at all, Vitor?" asked Stone.

Carvalho shook his head.

"No, sir. The Mon'golins were incredibly helpful, letting us fix our drive at their main space dock. If it weren't for their help and expertise, it would have taken us weeks, I'm sure of it. We couldn't have done it without them. They also gave us a healthy reserve of gluonite in case we leak some, like we did last time. We have enough to fully replenish the gluonite tanks. God forbid we run out somehow, touch wood."

Carvalho knocked on his desk with his knuckles. The desk wasn't wood but he did it nonetheless.

"I'm just running some final diagnostic tests, but I don't expect any problems at all. Give me five minutes and then we can take her out for a spin."

Carvalho was grinning widely.

"It's good to see you happy again, Vitor," said Stone.

"Well, it's contagious," Carvalho replied. "Seeing the renewed hope appear on the faces of our crew helped. We can really see the end now."

Stone nodded.

"I know, I just mentioned it to Suggs upstairs that we might even make it home for dinner, if all goes well," said Stone.

"I'm looking forward to heading to this little bistro I know in San Francisco. They make an incredible vegetable potpie. That's going to be my first order of business when we get back home."

"Well," said Stone standing up, "I'll let you get back to finishing up those diagnostics. I'll be on the bridge when you're ready. Come on up when you're done and we can crack the proverbial champagne bottle on the hull of the Falcon together."

"Will do," said Carvalho and his grin was still as wide as the horizon.

Stone went back up to the bridge. He entered and took command from Suggs.

"Anything of note?" he asked.

"Nothing to tell, Jack," said Suggs, "all's quiet and steady."

They watched the main viewer as they slipped by the other planets in the system. The planet of Mon'gol was no longer in sight. It was behind them, and the main viewer showed a small picture in picture of what they were leaving behind. A small dot blipped and finally disappeared. That was Mon'gol.

"Jenks and Kelly to the bridge," said Stone.

"On my way," said Jenks.

"Acknowledged, Jack," said Kelly.

"We've now cleared the Mon'gol's system, Captain. At your command we can enter into FTL flight," said Scot Free.

Scot Free was watching the main viewer with his hands at main helm's control. The viewer screen showed thousands of bright lights but none very big. They were now in open space. Space that was wide open even though it was dotted with more twinkling stars than you could count in a lifetime.

"Captain," said Carvalho through the intercom.

"Go ahead," said Stone.

"All diagnostic checks have been completed. Would you like the good news or the bad news first?"

Stone furrowed his brow.

"The bad news first, Vitor."

He was somewhat miffed. He didn't need any bad news now at this point. He just wanted to get them home dammit.

"Well, the bad news," said Vitor, "is that we spent five minutes running diagnostics that could've been spent at FTL."

Stone smiled.

"Okay, so what's the good news?"

"The good news, Captain, is that we're ready for lift off. All things are ready for launch, Houston," said Carvalho.

"Head on up to the bridge, Vitor, and would you mind stopping at mess and picking up some simuhol champagne and seven flutes?"

"Sure thing, Jack. I'll just be a minute."

And with that, Kelly and Jenks entered the bridge. Kelly sat next to Stone to his left and Jenks took a seat next to Suggs to his right.

"We're about to put the Falcon back into FTL, and I thought you might all like to be here for this new test run of the hyper drive."

"Very exciting," said Kelly rubbing her hands together.

"If all goes well, we could be home by around dinner time. I'm hoping," said Stone.

"It's been a long time, Captain, I look forward to seeing my wife again. Not that I don't enjoy your company," said Jenks.

They all smiled.

"Can't say I'll miss this part of space," said Kelly wistfully.

Suggs nodded.

"I didn't think my first tour would be this, um, difficult," said Suggs.

"Tell me about it," said Jenks. "In under two weeks we managed to lose half our crew. We're not getting home too soon, that's for sure."

"Agreed," said Stone. "I want the next exploration to be closer to home, maybe somewhere around the Milky Way."

Carvalho came in carrying a tray that held some champagne simuhol and seven flutes. He placed the tray on the helm's computer stand and gave the bottle to Stone to open.

"Shall I shake it?" he said grinning, pretending to start.

"No!" exclaimed Kelly.

Stone took off the cork's outer foil layer and twisted off the wire brace. He slowly pushed up on the cork until it suddenly flew off and hit the main viewer. They all chuckled. Stone poured the champagne into all seven flutes halfway. He handed the first one to Kelly.

"Ladies first," he said.

"Thank you."

Then he shared the remaining flutes around. To Suggs, Carvalho who had brought in the champagne, then to Jenks, followed by one for Scot Free.

"You can have this can't you?" he asked Scot Free.

"I can, though it will have no effect on me," he replied.

The penultimate flute he gave to Ensign Lawrence Tran who sat to Scot Free's right and was also a helmsman.

Stone held up his flute to his crew. He looked around at them as they all gathered round him and raised their glasses in return.

"To a quick and speedy flight home," he said. "And may it be uneventful."

"Hear, hear," said Suggs.

"I'll drink to that," said Carvalho.

And they all took turns clinking their glasses together. Scot Free took a polite sip from his flute before putting it back down on the tray.

"And now, let us engage hyper drive. Maximum hyper drive at your leisure, Lieutenant Scot Free," said Stone.

Scot Free sat down and Ensign Tran sat next to him.

"Engaging hyper drive engines, Captain. Three, two, one, engaged," said Scot Free.

The dots of twinkling light from the stars stretched out in front of them before turning into a sheet of light. The hyper drive engines engaged and they were instantaneously travelling faster than light. The stars zipped by them in technicolored brilliance.

They all went back to sitting down, placing their champagne flutes on the tray. Carvalho was to Kelly's left.

"How are the engines holding up?" asked Stone.

Carvalho tapped into his large monitor in front of him. A visual holographic screen appeared in front of him. He moved some of the displays around.

"All systems are functioning within ideal parameters, Captain. The engines are at full speed."

Stone nodded.

"Excellent," he said. "Excellent work, everyone."

"What is our scheduled ETA back to Earth?" Stone asked.

Carvalho tapped into his monitor. He looked at the screen and swiped the images away, one after the other. His forehead furrowed and his eyes squinted.

"This can't be," he said.

Stone looked at him quizzically. Carvalho tapped away quickly at his monitor, looking up as the images in front of him changed. He shook his head.

"I don't believe this Captain, it can't be," he said.

He shook his head and tapped at his monitor more aggressively. The holographic screen displayed a multitude of images, letters and numbers.

"What is it, Vitor?" said Stone.

Carvalho shook his head.

"I can't believe it," he said. "Let me check my numbers, Captain."

He went back to tapping into his monitor. Then he looked again at the screen. Then he swiped the images and the data back and forth.

"It makes no sense."

"What, Vitor, what?" demanded Stone.

Carvalho looked at his Captain.

"I don't know how to say this," he said.

"Just say it," said Stone.

"According to the computer's calculations and my calculations, it seems like it will take us about 120 thousand years to get home."

He looked forlorn. Kelly knitted her eyebrows together. Suggs looked at him with a raised eyebrow.

"What?" said Stone.

"120 thousand years to get home," Carvalho replied.

"Well, you must be wrong, or we're not traveling FTL," said Jenks.

Carvalho shook his head.

"No, according to the onboard computer we are traveling faster than light. In fact we're at maximum hyper drive which on these engines is 1 AU per sec."

"You're going to have to speak English," said Jenks.

"The computer tells me that we're traveling at the maximum speed possible for human engineered flight. Currently our maximum speed is right around one astronomical unit per second. I've double checked the computer readings and from what I can tell, we are zipping along at one astronomical unit per second."

"I'm still not following, Vitor," said Jenks.

"I think what he means to say is that we are traveling much faster than light," said Kelly, looking at Carvalho for acknowledgement. Carvalho nodded his head.

"Yes, that's right. Basically, we're traveling at around 540 billion kilometers per hour. The speed of light is roughly 1 billion kilometers per hour," said Carvalho.

"Then where's the problem?" asked Jenks. "We're traveling 540 times faster than light, right?"

Carvalho nodded.

"Yes," he said. "That's right, but the problem is, we're not traveling nearly fast enough to get home by dinner time."

"I'm afraid, Vitor, you're speaking above our pay grade here," said Stone. "I get the gist of what you're saying but can you put it in layman's terms?"

"I'll try," said Carvalho. "From what we know, and the onboard readings and diagnostics indicate that this is true, we are in the Virgo cluster."

They all nodded their understanding.

"Well, the Virgo cluster is really, really, really far away from Earth. If we traveled at the speed of light it would take us roughly 65 million years to get home from here. That's how far away from home we are," said Carvalho.

Again they all nodded.

"So," continued Carvalho, "we're traveling 540 times faster than light. If light takes 65 million years to get to Earth from here, then the Falcon, which is traveling 540 times faster than that, should be 540 times quicker. Dividing 65 million by 540 gives you 120 thousand years."

They all sat still silently for a moment. A somber mood fogged up the bridge.

"And you're certain that we are traveling as fast as possible?" asked Stone.

Carvalho nodded.

"I'm afraid so. I've checked and rechecked my calculations and the computer's calculations. I can't find any errors."

"Then how the hell did we get this far away from Earth in such a short time, less than two weeks?" asked Suggs.

"I don't have an answer for that just yet, Ty, I'm afraid," said Carvalho.

"Scot Free," said Stone.

"Yes Captain," answered Scot Free.

"Can you triple check these numbers and see if there is anything that we might be missing," said Stone. "No offense, Vitor."

"None taken, Captain," said Carvalho.

Kelly looked visibly shaken and upset. Her eyes were wet and damp.

"Then we'll never get back," she said.

Stone put his hand on her shoulder.

"Don't think like that," he said, "we have to find a way back. We did, after all, get here quickly, we just have to reverse engineer that journey to get us back."

"Captain," said Scot Free, "I have tripled checked the results and Commander Carvalho is correct. It will take us approximately 120 370 years and 135 days to get back to Earth at our current speed."

"You're certain?" asked Stone.

"Quite certain," said Scot Free looking steadily into his Captain's eyes.

"Well, then," said Stone, "our most pressing concern is finding out how we got here in under a day when we left Earth. I want everyone working on that, not just engineering. If we got here that quickly, we just have to find out how we did it, then reverse the process. I will not allow helplessness to take control of anyone on this ship. Yes, we've been through the ringer these past dozen days, but we're resilient and we're still here and we'll continue to fight until we no longer can."

Morale slowly started to lift in the bridge.

"Scot Free, I want you to spend every waking moment you can with Carvalho in engineering. And when he's sleeping I want you to carry on and figure out how we got here and how we can get back. And get back in the same timely manner that we got here in the first place.

"Yes, Captain," said Scot Free.

"Kelly, put your scientific background into this. Think of any ways that microbes, viruses, sub atomic particles are able to travel. There must be some method to how we got here and it might be found in science and medicine rather than engineering."

"I will, Jack," she said.

"And, Jenks," said Stone, "the martial arts, especially the philosophies behind them, might shed some light on how things move faster than they appear. See if you can't tease out anything from any of your martial arts' training that might give some light to this puzzle."

"Will do, Captain," said Jenks.

"You and I," said Stone to Suggs, "will man the bridge and put our collective brains to work on the problem, too."

Suggs nodded.

"Dismissed," said Stone. "See if we can't get to the bottom of this by the end of the day. I have faith in all of you. In us."

And with that, everyone left the bridge except for Stone, Suggs and Tran.

"Do you want us still to be traveling at FTL Captain?" asked Tran.

"Yes," said Stone, "it's not going to hinder our progress."

They watched the kaleidoscopic colors of the stars stream by like confetti. Stone had his chin between his thumb and forefinger, his mind drifted over the last several days. They had been banged up from the beginning. It was no wonder they were struggling now. He was also concerned about Kelly, she wasn't faring well.

"Suggs, I'm going down to Med Bay to see how Kelly is doing," Stone said.

"You bet, Captain," said Suggs.

"Keep those little gray cells working," Stone said as he left the bridge.

Down in Med Bay, Kelly was calibrating equipment and checking her supplies. She startled when Stone walked in.

"Sorry," he said, "didn't mean to give you a fright."

She put her hand over her chest and smiled thinly.

"It's okay," she said, "I guess I'm still a bit jumpy from our dealings with the Mon'gol Cable Wrathwon."

"I know," said Stone, "I've come to check up on you again, see how you're doing. You look well."

Stone took some medical supplies from her and helped her put them away.

"That's the great benefit of our medical technology. We can heal wounds, and bones and all sorts of things quite quickly and easily. The emotional scars are a little trickier."

Stone followed her into her office and they sat down. She sighed heavily.

"Who would've thought we'd end up in such a terrible mess?" she said.

Stone nodded grimly.

"I hear you. I know I've had a lot of tactical and military training, as have most of the men onboard here, but the amount and severity of the beatings we've taken has left us shaken."

"I hadn't even signed up for a military mission, Jack. I was originally scheduled for the SS Pax, except for a scheduling conflict that's the one I would have ended up on. Honestly, I have no desire for fighting and military tactics. I'm a pacifist, Jack, not a war doctor."

"I know," he said, "though I'm glad you're on here with me. I don't think you would have made it off the Pax alive."

Kelly looked down at her hands and nodded her head slowly.

"I'd just like to get home, Jack. The sooner the better."

"That's what we're working on," said Stone. "I'm sure between us we'll come up with an idea of how to make that happen."

Kelly looked at him and smiled again.

"You know," she said, "I was thinking about something earlier. The planet of Mon'gol wasn't all that far away from where we found Cable. At least relatively speaking."

Stone nodded.

"And yet Cable had said he came through a wormhole. He couldn't have, that must have been a lie."

Stone nodded.

"He was a liar and a murderer, I'd be surprised if anything he said was true."

"But what if," said Kelly, before trailing off.

"What?"

"I don't know, maybe you'll find this silly. But what if he had come through a wormhole?"

Kelly looked up at Stone to gauge his expression. Stone looked at her for a moment and then slowly nodded his head.

"You're thinking maybe we could travel back to Earth through a wormhole?"

"Well, it's just a thought," she said.

"I like it. It's the best thought I've heard all day. Let's take it to engineering and see what Carvalho and Scot Free think of it."

They got up and left Med Bay, headed for engineering. For the first time in many days, Kelly had a bounce in her step and the kindling fire of hope in her breast.

Scot Free and Carvalho were huddled in a corner by a large screen and monitor. They were animatedly discussing something. They stopped when they saw Stone and Kelly walk in.

"We have something we want to pass by you," said Stone, as Carvalho was about to speak.

"You first, Vitor," said Stone.

"No, sorry Captain, you go ahead, we can wait," said Carvalho.

"Okay," said Stone, turning to Kelly, "it's your idea, explain it to them."

"Well, I don't know if it's feasible," said Kelly, "but I was thinking about Cable earlier, when Jack came in to see how I was doing. Anyway, I remember him saying how he came through a wormhole. But that was obviously a lie because we've just come back from Mon'gol and it wasn't that far from where we found that bastard. I didn't really think much of it until our conversation earlier about getting home. I'm wondering if it's possible to get back to Earth through one of these wormholes?"

Carvalho nodded.

"Tell them," he said to Scot Free.

"Well, Captain, Commander," said Scot Free, addressing both Kelly and Stone, "we've been going through all the scientific knowledge and engineering knowledge that Commander Carvalho and I have. It appears that just like Commander Kelly suggests, the only viable option to get back to Earth in a timely fashion is going to be through natural events like a wormhole."

Kelly smiled.

"That's great," she said.

"It is and it isn't," said Carvalho. "As Scot Free mentioned, from all the information we've been able to sift through, a wormhole seems like the only viable method to get us home. But, and this is a big but, it is not without its risks."

"All right then, let's get the first officers to the briefing room and we can discuss it and make a decision then," said Stone.

As they headed up to engineering, Stone called on Jenks and Suggs to meet him there.

They all took their seats around the large oval table.

"It appears we have found a way to get us home," said Stone, "but we've all gathered here because I want this to be a unanimous decision. There are risks, as Carvalho will mention. With any dissenting opinion we'll have to seek another way or make it back more slowly than we'd like. Carvalho, please give us your best professional opinion of success and risks."

Carvalho stood up and walked to the wall where a computer monitor and screen was placed. He faced his fellow officers.

"It appears that great minds think alike," he said, smiling and trying for a bit of levity. "Aimee came up with this idea, likely at around the same time that Scot Free and I were discussing it and she and Jack came to us with it. Basically, the idea is that we'll use a wormhole to get us home."

Carvalho tapped on the monitor and an image of a wormhole appeared on the screen.

"We have a pretty good understanding of how wormholes work. I think the easiest way to explain it to you is like this. If you imagine space or the universe to be a thin blanket, then what a wormhole does is attach one point of the blanket to another."

He showed how this might work on the screen. The blanket pinched up from two different ends and touched in the middle.

"So in essence," he continued, "you're able to travel great distances in a matter of seconds or minutes, depending on the wormhole and the distance traveled. Theoretically, you could travel from one end of the universe to the other in mere minutes, if they were attached by a wormhole."

"So it's like a tube then?" asked Suggs.

"In a manner of speaking," said Carvalho.

"Then let's do this," said Jenks, "what's the problem?"

Carvalho smiled.

"Yes," he said. "What are the problems? There are several. This schematic I've just shown you is a nice and neat way of looking at it. These two ends of the blankets meet nicely and neatly, you start at one end of the wormhole and you end up millions of light years away on the other end. The problem is, you don't know where the other end, ends up."

"So we send a probe," said Suggs.

"There is a problem with that too," said Carvalho. "Most wormholes are highly dynamic. Imagine you've coiled up a garden hose and you suddenly open up the water valve to maximum. I'm sure you've all seen this, the end of the hose starts whipping about violently. We believe that's how most wormholes work. You can enter just seconds apart and end up thousands and millions of light years away from each other. Additionally, most wormholes open up for just a fraction of a second. Some for several seconds and very few are open for more than a few minutes at a time. So the chances are, if you find one you have to decide quickly if you're going to take it."

The faces around the table weren't looking very sunny anymore.

"There is one other consideration we should bear in mind. Some wormholes; and we aren't certain how many, it may be as many as half of them, bend not only space, but also time."

"What does that mean?" asked Kelly.

"Well it means; that not only can you be spat out the other end of a wormhole millions of light years from your current position, which is what we want, but you could also be spat out years into the future or back into the past."

"How many years?" asked Suggs.

"We don't know. But theoretically, you could be pushed thousands, maybe millions of years into the past or future."

"Is there anything else?" asked Stone.

"I'd just like to leave you with my final, professional thoughts on this. Scot Free and I have looked at all the angles. We can't see how to get back to Earth in under a hundred thousand years without some miracle or technological breakthrough that we might encounter. The only way we can make it is through a wormhole. I'd sooner take my chances with a wormhole, but there are risks. Scot Free has calculated those risks. Scot Free."

"If we analyze the direction of the wormhole before we enter it, we can likely be 73 percent certain it will take us in the direction we want," said Scot Free. "However, we can't determine if a specific wormhole is bending time as well as space. From the knowledge that humans have and the knowledge I've gathered from my builders which I don't have much access to, I'm fairly certain the chances of a wormhole bending both space and time is 13 percent."

"I can live with those odds," said Suggs.

"I have a question," said Jenks. "If this is how we got here in the first place, why don't we access the computer logs and retrace the wormholes we took to get here?"

"That's a great question," said Carvalho. "Firstly, I'm not certain how we got here. The more I think about it, the more I believe that we had to get here via wormholes or some other yet to be discovered phenomenon. Having intimate knowledge with our understanding of space travel I'd say we traveled via wormholes. However, here's the thing. The computer was either instructed not to create records of the course it took, which perhaps Star Ship Command preprogrammed, or that data has been lost during one of our many skirmishes. Neither Scot Free or I can find any of this information."

"So you're saying that Star Ship Command might have sent us here covertly, using technology that they weren't willing to share?" asked Jenks.

"It is one of the possibilities," said Carvalho, "though I personally think that what has happened is that in all the fighting, and all the damage the ship has taken, some of our data has been corrupted. So the data is, or was there, but is no longer available to us."

"That still doesn't explain why this information wasn't handed to us during the briefing. Sounds more like we've been sent out here like guinea pigs," said Jenks, getting angry as the thought dawned on him.

Jack put up his hand to stop them.

"This is all speculation. What we have to concern ourselves with at the moment is the matter at hand, which is how do we get back home. This is our primary concern and it seems that the only option available to us is the use of wormholes," said Stone.

"Jack," said Jenks, "we've known each other a long time. This is the first time that SSC has been less than forthright. If they were sending us so far into outer space that we had to use untested or new technology, then why would they hold that from us? It means they sent us on a suicide mission without our knowledge or consent. You can be sure that makes me mad as hell."

Jack didn't say anything, he was deep in thought.

"He has a point, Jack," said Suggs.

Kelly nodded, as did Carvalho.

"You know Captain, it is somewhat suspicious. It's one thing to suggest that the computer's memory banks have been damaged. That's highly unlikely with the triple redundancies in place. But let's say that's the case," said Carvalho, "surely, with such new methods of space/time travel, they would have briefed us intensely on it?"

Jack clasped his hands in front of him for a moment. Steepling them and resting his chin on his fingertips. He pinched his lips together.

"I hear what you are all saying. I'm not saying it is without merit. But it is speculation at this point, even if it is intelligent speculation. I can't believe that Admiral Vitran would send me, send us, out here without full disclosure. Until we can get back and ask these questions, we need to move forward. Your concerns are valid but there is nothing we can do here on the outer edges of the Virgo Cluster, 65 odd million light years from Earth. We might as well be railing against the heavens," said Stone.

Jenks shook his head, he was still upset.

"Okay," said Suggs, "getting back on track. Let me see if I understand this. We have to first find a wormhole and then we have to determine if it is heading in the right direction. And if it is, we can only be, at best, 73 percent certain of that. And if we get the 73 percent certainty right, we still have a 13 percent chance of ending up out of sync in some other time period. Do I understand this correctly?"

"That is a rudimentary, crude but accurate understanding," said Scot Free.

"My next question then, is how many wormholes are there out there?" asked Suggs.

"That's hard to say for certain, Ty. Much like gluonite, some areas of space could be heavily populated with wormholes and in other areas it might be like looking for a needle in a haystack. Humanity is new to the Virgo Cluster. We're the first here. We haven't been looking for wormholes so we can't say how many we might encounter out here. Furthermore, we have to drop out of FTL in order to scan for them effectively. Even at maximum LUX drive, we're still quite vulnerable to any malevolence that might be out there to prey on us. But it's a chance we have to take," said Carvalho.

"I'll also have to make changes to our scanners so that they can pick up the signature electro-photonic pulse that wormholes give off while they're open. But that should be relatively easy," said Scot Free.

They all sat in silence for a while contemplating their options.

"I like them apples," said Suggs. "I vote we give it a try. I certainly don't want to die out here today, tomorrow, or of old age trying to make our way back home without putting in our best efforts. Let's take the best chances and the necessary risks to get us back. I don't want to spend my last days in regret. That's my vote."

Stone looked at Jenks.

"Sure," he said, "let's go for it. I live for the action, the unknown."

Stone then looked at Kelly. She looked back at him and tried to smile bravely. It slipped off her face rather easily. She nodded.

"Yes," she said, "me, too. Let's try it."

She looked back down at her hands in her lap.

Stone looked at Carvalho.

"Count me in, Jack. I don't think we have any other choices. If we take the necessary precautions, I believe our chances of success are high," said Carvalho.

"And what about you, Lieutenant Scot Free, our friend from a galaxy far, far away."

"It makes no difference to me, Captain. I am here to serve under your command and help you make it home safely," said Scot Free.

"But your opinion still counts," said Stone.

"Then I opine we attempt to worm our way home." Suggs smiled.

"And you Jack, the last vote is yours," said Kelly.

"I'm an adventurer," he said, "and this sounds like one hell of an adventure. Let's go for it."

"We're unanimous," said Suggs.

"Okay, we're all going to the bridge. Scot Free, I want you to make the necessary adjustments to our scanners and find us a wormhole asap."

"Right you are, Captain," said Scot Free.

They made their way back to the bridge. Scot Free took his seat and made the adjustments to the scanners. It only took about five minutes. Ensign Tran dropped them out of warp.

"We're at full LUX speed, Captain," said Tran.

"Good," said Stone. "Now we look for that needle in the haystack."

They were all seated in their chairs around the Captain. Scot Free and Ensign Tran were in front facing the main viewer. The main viewer showed the main view of what was coming up as if they could see it with their own eyes. In the corner of the main viewer was another view, this one was a 360 degree view of space around the SS Falcon. It looked similar to a radar image. In the center was the Falcon and emanating from it was a blue fog that stretched out into a 3D circle and faded away as it completed one scan. Then it started over and over again.

"The image of a wormhole will look very much like a red or orange squiggle," said Scot Free. "That's what we're looking for."

And so they all watched and waited on tenterhooks, for what seemed like days. They were traveling at maximum LUX speed which was roughly 99 percent the speed of light. Almost 300 thousand kilometers per second were whizzing by at what looked like a very leisurely pace.

"Keep long distance scans for any anomalies or spaceships," said Stone.

"Aye, Captain," said Tran.

And then they saw it, after about a half hour of staring into the viewer and seeing nothing of note, there was a faint blip of orange at the very outer edges of the scanning range, at about eleven o' clock. They were flying away from it.

"What's that?" said Suggs, pointing to the fading blip.

"That looks like a wormhole," said Carvalho. "Scot Free, can you confirm."

Scot Free made some adjustments to the calibrations and the blip danced and squiggled brighter.

"Yes, Commander, that looks like a wormhole," confirmed Scot Free.

There was chatter and applause around the bridge.

"How far away?" asked Stone.

"Just over a half billion kilometers, Captain," said Scot Free.

"Take us to it, Ensign," said Stone.

"Right away, Captain," replied Tran. "We should get there in about thirty minutes."

And those thirty minutes felt like thirty hours to the bridge crew of the Star Ship Falcon. They took position about a million kilometers from the wormhole's opening.

"Send a probe in first to take measurements and determine if this is a good wormhole for us," said Stone, hoping it was a stable and long lasting wormhole.

Scot Free released a probe that made its way to the wormhole. It disappeared inside its mirrored opening within just a few seconds. They waited until it streamed data back to them until it finally stopped sending any more.

Scot Free looked at the data and ran some diagnostics.

"This one makes the cut Captain. I can say with roughly 73 percent certainty that it should get us closer to Earth than we are now," said Scot Free. "However, it is becoming unstable and will be unusable in 97 seconds."

"Well, this is our chance, then," said Stone, looking around at his colleagues. "Everybody in?"

They all nodded. Stone tapped at his monitor in front of him.

"This is the Captain speaking. We are about to enter a wormhole to get us home quicker. The ride may be a little bumpy. Secure, what you can. We enter in thirty seconds."

Stone ended the transmission.

"Ensign, take us into that wormhole in thirty seconds," said Stone.

"Aye, Captain."

"Jenks, shields at maximum," said Stone.

Jenks tapped at the monitor in front of him. The bridge dimmed and a red glow filled the ship on all decks. Shields at maximum always engaged red alert.

"Shields enabled, Captain," said Jenks.

They entered the wormhole and a lit tunnel swarmed around them as if they were zipping down a long and winding water slide tube. The light was blues and greens and whites and seemed to be liquid. The entry and the travel was smooth and not bumpy at all. Some static light, like electricity, lit up the ship's outer shields and inside the bridge, lightning appeared to engulf Scot Free for a fraction of a second. It happened too fast for anyone to notice.

And then, less than a minute later they slipped out of the wet wormhole, still traveling at LUX speed.

"All stop," said Stone.

"All stop, Captain," came Tran's reply.

They looked around. Space looked eerily familiar. That was the thing with deep, black space. You couldn't tell it apart from one light year to the next unless you knew of any anomalies in the area.

"Coordinates?" asked Stone, looking at the main viewer.

Scot Free's neck and head shook as if it had vibrated and his eyes twitched.

"Yes, Captain, we are three million light years from Earth. We have traveled approximately 62 million light years."

Scot Free's head shook again, and his arm jumped involuntarily.

"Lieutenant, are you okay?" asked Stone.

Scot Free did not look round. He did not answer Captain Stone, instead, he fell off his chair and landed immobile on the floor.

EARTH RISE

"What on Earth!" exclaimed Captain Stone.

He walked over to Scot Free and knelt down by him. He went to touch him, to gently shake him on the shoulder. As he did he was zapped by a tremendous electrical charge that shot him off Scot Free violently. Captain Stone landed a few feet away, on his back. He shook his head.

"Captain!" yelled Suggs, as he ran up to him. "Captain, are you okay?"

Suggs knelt down by Stone and touched him carefully on the shoulder. Stone looked up at him and slowly shook his head.

"I feel fine, though that was quite a shock," said Stone.

Suggs helped Stone get up from the floor. Jenks came over to his Captain and First Officer. Jenks had his pulsar trained on Scot Free. Scot Free was twitching on the floor in front of them.

"Doctor, can you scan him? See what's wrong with him," said Stone.

Kelly came up to Scot Free and knelt down by him. She took out her medscanner and slowly waved it over him. She shook her head.

"I don't understand his makeup fully, but his bio-plasmatic membranes are lighting up like Christmas trees," she said.

"What does it mean?" asked Stone.

Stone, Jenks and Suggs came up to Scot Free and knelt beside the doctor. Stone waved Jenks' pulsar away and he holstered it.

"Nobody should touch him," said Kelly, "until I can figure out what has happened to him."

She continued to scan him as Scot Free lay there, vibrating every so often like some old robot whose batteries were faltering.

"What can we do doctor?" asked Suggs.

Kelly turned to look at him and closed her medscanner.

"I don't think there is very much we can do for him right now. As I said, I don't fully understand his bio-plasmatic electrical membranes. But from what I can tell, he has encountered some sort of violent, electrical or photonic charge. I'm reading a thousand fold increase in his energy output from what it should normally be."

"Is there any danger to us?" asked Jenks.

"I can't tell for sure. But this kind of electrical charge would kill a human. I just don't know if he can survive," said Kelly.

"Doctor," said Stone, "perhaps you can help him better in Med Bay. I'll have O'Reilly stream him right to you."

Kelly got up and left the bridge via the lift. Stone tapped his c-star badge.

"Transit," he said.

"Transit here, Captain," said O'Reilly.

"Chief, I have Lieutenant Scot Free here who has been hit with some sort of electrical charge. We need him streamed to Med Bay on the double."

"Right away, Captain," said O'Reilly.

Stone, Suggs and Carvalho who had now also come up to see what was going on with Scot Free, and Jenks backed away to give Transit space to lock in on Scot Free. They watched as the streaming process started, but it didn't get anywhere. Scot Free sparkled and sparked, but he didn't dematerialize out of the bridge. Stone waited for several seconds. They all watched, but nothing happened.

"O'Reilly, fast as you can please," said Stone.

"Captain, I can't get a lock on his bio-pattern. Something is interfering with letting me lock in on him."

"Keep trying," said Stone.

And the sparkling Scot Free sparkled and sparked even more violently.

"Captain, I'm getting a dangerous amount of feedback here. It might blow our buffers," said O'Reilly.

"Captain," said Carvalho, "doesn't look like it's helping Scot Free either."

Stone nodded.

"Very well, O'Reilly," said Stone. "Disengage streaming."

"Aye, Captain," said O'Reilly.

Scot Free stopped sparking and the sparkles ceased. To the crew on the bridge, Scot Free looked like his old self. They could not see the energy discharge he was emanating as Commander Kelly had said he was. His twitching was slowly becoming less pronounced.

"I'll help him to Med Bay, Captain," said Carvalho.

Carvalho approached Scot Free and put his hands down under him to try and lift him up.

"No, don't!" said Stone.

But it was too late. A static discharge violently ejected Carvalho from Scot Free's body. And just like what had happened with Stone earlier, Carvalho found himself on his back a few feet away. Dazed and confused but not injured.

Stone went up to him and helped pull him up.

"You forgot what happened to me," he said to his Engineering Officer.

Carvalho nodded, pressed his shirt down and rolled his head.

"Yes, I had a momentary lapse in judgment. I also forgot just how heavy Scot Free is. What was I thinking? There is no way in hell I could carry him by myself."

Stone smiled at Carvalho.

"You're okay?" he asked.

Carvalho nodded.

"Surprisingly. That was quite the shock but I feel fine," said Carvalho.

"Good. I'd still like you to go and get checked by the doctor," said Stone. "Perhaps from any residual charge left on you, she can figure out what we're dealing with."

Carvalho nodded.

"Very well, Jack, but shouldn't you come, too?" Carvalho asked.

Stone smiled at him.

"No, if the doctor thinks I need to come and see her after she's seen you then I will," said Stone.

Carvalho left the bridge to make his way to Med Bay.

"Anyone have any thoughts?" asked Stone, looking around at the remaining bridge crew.

He was met with glum faces.

"We need Scot Free's help in order to find the next wormhole to take. Damn, this is not helpful," Stone said to himself.

Stone looked at Scot Free and rubbed his own chin. He couldn't touch him to help him, and he couldn't figure out what to do. Slowly though, Scot Free came to. He got himself up to a sitting position and looked around at his surroundings. He then got up to standing.

"Sorry, Captain," said Scot Free, "something came over me. I have no idea why I was on the floor."

"You gave us all quite a scare," said Stone. "Is everything all right."

Scot Free took a moment to run diagnostics on himself. There were no overt anomalies that he could pick out, so he nodded at his Captain.

"I appear to be fit as a fiddle," he said, "though I have no idea what happened. Can you enlighten me Captain?"

"I'm not sure, myself, what happened," said Stone. "We entered the wormhole and everything appeared to be going much more smoothly than we anticipated. In fact it was without incident. However, just as we exited, your head seemed to shake, and then the next moment you fell to the floor, where you twitched and shook intermittently. None of us could tell that anything was wrong with you, but Commander Kelly said you were lit up like a Christmas tree."

"A Christmas tree, Captain?" asked Scot Free.

Stone nodded.

"Yes, it appears you were hit with a large amount of electrical or photonic discharge of some sort. You have no information about that?" asked Stone.

Again, Scot Free took a moment to run some further tests. He again shook his head.

"No, Captain, strangely, it appears that my memory has been erased for the last three minutes and thirty three seconds," said Scot Free.

"But you feel fine?" asked Stone

"Yes, Captain, fit as a fiddle, as I said," Scot Free replied.

"I'd still like to have you checked over by Doctor Kelly, just to be sure," said Stone.

"Right away, Captain," said Scot Free as he left the bridge.

"Med Bay," said Stone.

"Kelly here, Captain," came the reply.

"I've sent both Carvalho and Scot Free to you for a scan. Let me know if you find anything at all. Even the smallest anomaly," said Stone.

"Yes, Captain," said Kelly. "I've just finished running a thorough diagnostic check on Vitor and he is quite healthy. The only thing I picked up was a small residual electrical impulse charge, but it doesn't appear to have been harmful. It's quite remarkable actually, Jack. This impulse of whatever it was, electric, photonic, or otherwise, appears to have been extremely powerful but at the same time harmless to human tissue."

"Glad to hear it. Let's hope it will be found to be equally harmless to Scot Free's tissues," said Stone.

"I'll keep you informed, Captain," said Kelly.

The SS Falcon hung like a Christmas tree bauble in the vast emptiness of black space. The twinkling stars like Christmas tree lights in the distance. At least they were closer to home. Substantially closer, though they still needed another wormhole or two before they might get back to Earth within the next few weeks or months. But so far, things were looking good for a change.

Captain Jack Stone went and sat back in his Captain's chair. Suggs sat to his right.

"Ensign Tran," said Stone.

"Yes, Captain," said Tran swiveling his chair around to see the Captain.

"Did you happen to notice anything strange with Lieutenant Scot Free before, during or after we entered the wormhole?" asked Stone.

Tran took a moment to think about the events. Then he shook his head.

"No sir, I'm afraid I didn't notice anything unusual at all. The computer wasn't reading any anomalies, and our travel through the wormhole was uneventful. I only noticed something strange when Lieutenant Scot Free fell to the floor. Nothing before that Captain."

"Very well," said Stone. "Thank you, Ensign."

Tran turned back to his station and looked at the main viewer. Stone turned to Suggs.

"What do you think?" Stone asked.

"I think it was certainly strange and odd behavior, but he appears to be fine. Perhaps it was just some sort of anomaly."

"Perhaps," said Stone, "but we were at red alert, full shields. How did anything get through to attack Scot Free? And if it did, how come it didn't affect us?"

"We can't answer that for right now, Jack. But this is the first time we've been through a wormhole. This is all new. Perhaps there is a type of energy within wormholes we aren't aware of that can easily enter our shields and affect bio-electrical plasmatic membranes like Scot Free's, but not our own tissues," said Suggs.

Stone nodded.

"Perhaps it would be prudent to have Scot Free turn himself off before we enter the next wormhole, if there is a real concern of this happening again," said Suggs.

"Good idea, Ty," said Stone, "if he is fit for duty."

A short time later, Scot Free returned to the bridge. He seemed normal to both Captain Stone and Commander Suggs.

"What's the word?" asked Stone.

"Nothing abnormal Captain," replied Scot Free. "Doctor Kelly gave me a clean bill of health. The energy fluctuation she noticed earlier seems to have all but subsided. Personally, I feel fine."

Stone nodded.

"Kelly," he said.

"Kelly here, Captain."

"You were going to give me an update. I see Lieutenant Scot Free has arrived on the bridge. Can you explain," said Stone. He sounded a little testy.

"Sorry, Captain, my oversight," said Kelly. "I've given Lieutenant Scot Free a thorough look and he has a clean bill of health. If there is anything wrong with him, I can't tell what it is with our technologies. He seems fine. There is only the smallest residue of electrical discharge that I can find on him. I believe he is fit for duty."

"Thank you, doctor," said Stone.

Stone walked up to Scot Free. He put his hand on his shoulder. Stone was not ejected off him like last time. Indeed, the android seemed normal.

"Yes, Captain?" asked Stone.

"Nothing," said Stone, smiling at him. "Carry on; find us another wormhole if you can."

"Certainly, sir," said Scot Free.

Scot Free went back to his station and sat down. As soon as he did, his head jerked again. Stone noticed.

"Everything all right, Lieutenant?" asked Stone.

"Yes, Captain," said Scot Free without looking around at his Captain.

Scot Free tapped into the computer at his station. Moments later they had jumped to FTL. Stone noticed.

"Lieutenant, we cannot find wormholes at faster than light speed," said Stone.

"Understood, Captain," said Scot Free.

And they continued heading away from the wormhole at maximum hyper drive speeds. Stone looked at Suggs and frowned. Suggs looked concerned.

"Lieutenant!" said Stone, "drop us out of hyper drive this instance."

Scot Free did not respond. Stone got up from his chair and walked over to where Scot Free was sitting.

"Lieutenant," he said, "I gave you a direct order."

Scot Free still did not acknowledge his Captain. Stone put his hand on Scot Free's shoulder to turn him around. Instead, he was thrown off him by the same charge he had experienced earlier. He landed a few feet away, on his back again, dazed but uninjured. Stone got up and returned to his chair. Suggs looked at Stone.

"I'll take care of this myself," Stone said.

He tapped into the terminal attached to his chair. Nothing happened.

"That's odd," said Stone. "Suggs, shut out Scot Free, it appears I can't access the system."

Suggs tapped into his terminal with the same effect.

"I seem to be shut out, too, Captain," he said.

"Computer," said Stone.

"Yes, Captain," came the computer's reply.

"Return all helm control to the Captain and the Captain alone. Authorization Jack Stone Alpha 0377," said Stone.

"Unable to comply," said the computer.

"Why not?" demanded Stone.

"Authorization protocols have been overwritten," said the computer.

"Lieutenant, stop this nonsense this instant," said Stone.

Scot Free turned around and looked at Captain Stone.

"Sorry, Captain, I am unable to do that," he said.

"Listen, Lieutenant," said Stone, "I want you to stop this nonsense right now. Step away from your console."

Instead, Scot Free swiveled back to face his terminal and he typed furiously at the controls. He was exceedingly fast. Stone was furious now.

"Computer," said Stone, "erect a level ten force field around Lieutenant Scot Free."

"Unable to comply," came the reply.

"Computer, is there anything you can comply with on my command?" asked Stone.

"No, Captain," came the reply. "Your authorization has been circumvented and you are no longer in command."

"By who's authorization!" demanded Stone.

"Star Ship Command," replied the computer.

"Captain," said Jenks. "If I may."

Jenks had his pulsar out and trained on Scot Free. Stone raised his hand for a moment.

"I've just about had enough of this," said Stone. "Lieutenant Scot Free, this is your last warning. Disengage hyper drive and remove yourself from your station."

It was as if Scot Free was deaf. He ignored his Captain and continued working away furiously at his terminal. Stone looked over at Jenks and nodded. Jenks fired his pulsar at a moderate intensity. Powerful enough to immobilize most life forms, including Scot Free, without causing serious injury. As the pulsar beam hit Scot Free a force field erupted around him and the pulse was easily absorbed. Scot Free didn't notice.

"Full setting of photonic pulse," said Stone.

"That will vaporize him, Captain," said Jenks.

Stone was grim faced and severe.

"I am aware of that, Commander. We have given him every opportunity. Fire when ready," said Stone.

He wasn't happy about giving this order. They needed Scot Free in order to find another wormhole and get home. But more importantly he needed to gain control of the ship again. Without that, they'd never get home. And with each passing second they were traveling millions of kilometers in the wrong direction. Stone was confident that Carvalho could figure out how to find additionally needed wormholes. Regardless of whether Scot Free had erased the wormhole calibrations or not.

Commander Timothy Jenks steadied his pulsar. He thumbed the biometric safety override and aimed at Scot Free. He pursed his lips. Then he fired. The powerful photonic pulse smashed against Scot Free. But it smashed against him like waves against granite rock. It had absolutely no affect. Scot Free appeared to be unaware.

"Again," said Stone.

Jenks checked his pulsar's settings. They were at maximum. He aimed and fired again. Nothing, not the slightest budge or movement came from Scot Free. Stone was incensed. He came up to Scot Free and grabbed him by the shoulders and tried to shake him. This time he was not ejected by some force field, and yet at the same time he was unable to move Scot Free an inch.

Scot Free finished madly tapping away at the terminal and turned around to face Stone. Stone backed away a couple of feet as Scot Free stood up. There was something odd about him. Scot Free had a faraway stare. He seemed, if he were human, to be in some sort of trance or dream state. He opened his mouth and a high pitched shriek came out. The bridge crew had to cover their ears. After a few seconds the noise stopped, and Scot Free spoke, but it was not his voice, it sounded like a child talking through a robot.

"We apologize," said Scot Free. "We did not mean to inconvenience you. We are simply going home."

"Who are you?" demanded Stone.

"We are Phostrans from planet Phostras," said Scot Free.

"What have you done to my Lieutenant and this ship?" asked Stone.

"We were trapped in the time tunnel which you call a wormhole. We were placed as prisoners there by the Diabolans. They captured us and kept us prisoner in that time tunnel because they thought it would stabilize the time tunnel and allow them easy and quick access to pillage the adjacent galaxies."

Jenks put away his pulsar and came up to Stone's side.

"What do you want with us?" asked Jenks.

"We want nothing of you, other than the use of your ship to take us home to our planet Phostras. We have been trapped for three tremins. This is about three hundred of your years. We have been unable to escape until your android came by. His bio-plasmatic electrical membranes were compatible with our life form and we were able to hitch a ride on him as you entered the time tunnel."

"Where is your home, this Phostras?" asked Stone.

"It is close by. We will be there in fewer than thirty of your minutes at current speed. If you allow us to return safely home, we will provide you with details on where to find more time tunnels to get yourselves home."

Stone looked at Scot Free who still seemed half asleep. He nodded.

"It appears we don't have much of a choice," said Stone.

"No, you do not. But we are grateful for your hospitality," said Scot Free.

"Will you at least give me my Lieutenant back, my android?" asked Stone.

"You must understand, we do not trust humanoids very easily. The Diabolans were humanoid like you and they trapped us and kept us enslaved in that time tunnel. If we give you back your android you must give us your word you will allow us to get home."

Stone nodded.

"I give you my word. It doesn't appear that we have any choice in this matter in any event. Perhaps this can be the start of a new relationship between humanity and your species."

"Perhaps," said Scot Free.

And with that, two cloud-like forms of electricity emanated from Scot Free and appeared floating above him.

"Captain," said Scot Free confused.

"Yes, Leiutenant," said Stone.

"I feel as though I should apologize," said Scot Free.

"Yes, indeed. Though it appears you were used without your consent," said Stone.

"Yes... I was," said Scot Free. "Interesting, these beings do not have malevolent intent. Rather, they distrust bipedal humanoids, so it appears, and they just wanted to hitch a ride home. You can't blame them after having been trapped for over three hundred years. Can you?"

"No, I suppose you can't. But their manners could use some fine tuning. Glad to have you back, Lieutenant," said Stone.

Scot Free sat back down at his terminal and Stone went back to his chair where he sat down. Jenks joined him to his left and Carvalho sat back down on his right, one up from Suggs.

"Computer, has command of this ship been returned to me?" asked Stone.

"It has," came the reply.

"What do you want to do?" asked Suggs.

"Get our guests home and then onward to Earth," said Stone.

The SS Falcon soon dropped out of FTL and came to a full stop. They were close to a gigantic gaseous planet that lit up and blinked with what appeared to be electrical charges.

"Scot Free, can you tell if this is Phostras?" asked Stone.

Scot Free looked at the terminal.

"It appears to be so, Captain," he said. "These are the coordinates that I entered when I was, how can I say this, not myself."

Stone nodded.

"Good," he said. "Perhaps our guests will be so kind as to disembark."

The two clouds of electricity, the Phostrans disappeared into the terminal by Scot Free. Moments later, text appeared on the main viewer.

"We are grateful for your kindness. We will now leave you," it said.

It was followed by a set of coordinates indicating a time tunnel. The two clouds of electricity reappeared from the terminal and then vanished in a twinkling of light.

"Computer," said Stone, "any sign of our former guests?"

"They are no longer aboard the SS Falcon," replied the computer.

"Good," said Stone. "Perhaps we can get ourselves home now. Ensign, take us to those coordinates."

"Yes, sir," said Ensign Tran.

The Phostrans had not lied. The wormhole was close by, taking no more than twenty minutes at FTL. Tran dropped them out of hyper drive flight close by the wormhole. On the main viewer they could see its glimmering wet face.

"Scot Free, could you be so kind as to analyze this wormhole for us to see if it is indeed a viable one," said Stone.

"Right away, Captain," answered Scot Free.

Scot Free sent a probe off into the wormhole. It entered within several seconds, and for a few seconds it sent back analysis. Scot Free tabulated the results.

"Captain, this wormhole is in the right direction. At least from what I can tell, there is a 73 percent chance that we'll end up closer to Earth. As to maintaining our time continuum, that remains to be seen, but the chances are good. You'll recall that our best estimates suggest that a wormhole is likely to bend both space and time only 13 percent of the time."

Stone nodded.

"Understood," he said. "How stable is this wormhole?"

"It is reasonably stable, Captain," answered Scot Free. "More stable than the last one. I believe we have seven or more minutes before it disappears again."

"Good," said Stone.

Stone tapped into his terminal.

"Commander Kelly to the bridge," he said.

"On my way, Captain," she replied.

They waited for Kelly to enter the bridge.

"It appears we have found our next wormhole," said Stone. "Everyone willing to give it a try?"

He looked around at the bridge crew, made up mostly of his officers. Everyone nodded.

"To home, and not through the park, Captain," said Suggs, grinning.

Stone tapped into the terminal attached to his chair.

"This is the Captain speaking," he said. "We are about to enter our second wormhole. We don't expect it to be any different than the first, but to be sure, please fasten anything that might need fastening. We will enter in sixty seconds."

Kelly came and took her seat with the other officers of the SS Falcon. She was seated to Jenks left.

"Jenks," said Stone, "shields to maximum just to be sure."

Jenks nodded and tapped at his terminal.

"Shields are at maximum, Captain."

They waited for the full sixty seconds to count down.

"Scot Free," said Stone, "please take us into the wormhole."

"Aye, Captain," answered Scot Free.

The SS Falcon, under LUX power, entered the wormhole. The tunnel swarmed with multi-colored lights, mostly greens and blues. However, this time the trip was bumpier for some reason and seemed to go on longer. The wormhole kept them within her wet grip longer than seemed necessary. They exited after fifty three seconds.

"All stop," said Stone.

Scot Free bought the ship to a stop. And tapped into his console to determine exactly where they were.

"Good news, Captain," said Scot Free.

"Go on," said Stone.

"It appears that we have hit the lottery. We are literally less than ten hours away from Earth at LUX speed," said Scot Free.

There was a round of applause from the bridge crew. Stone smiled warmly. Kelly clutched her hands together in relief.

"That is good news," said Stone. "Where exactly are we?"

Scot Free tapped into his terminal and on the main viewer an image came up of the solar system.

"As you can see from the viewer, Captain," said Scot Free, "we are outside Pluto's orbit at approximately 9.8 billion kilometers from Earth."

There were more congratulations and pats on the back.

"Good work, Lieutenant," said Stone. "Ensign Tran, take us to half slip knot speed which should get us to earth within twenty minutes, correct?"

Tran entered the coordinates into the terminal and engaged hyper drive slip knot speed.

"Arrival time at Space Station Sputnik should be 19 minutes and 37 seconds, Captain, after we drop out of FTL on the dark side of the moon."

"Well done, Captain," said Suggs.

"Thank you," said Kelly.

Jenks thumped Stone on the upper shoulder, grinning broadly. Stone again tapped into his terminal.

"This is your Captain speaking. We have arrived at our solar system. We are scheduled to dock with the space station in about twenty minutes. Please begin preparing for debarkation."

"There are going to be some very happy crew to hear that message, Captain," said Suggs.

"I sure hope so," said Stone, "we might just make it home in time for dinner."

The nineteen minute trip felt like it had taken as long as the thirteen days they had been gone. But all throughout the ship toasts were being shared and beaming, happy faces walked the corridors on buoyant steps. Steven Fouse made his way to Med Bay where Janice Qualls was packing some of her things. They embraced.

"Thank God we've finally made it home," he said to her as he held her at arm's length after kissing her.

"I know, I can't wait to set foot on terra firma again," Janice said smiling happily.

"Hey," said Steven, "how about joining me for dinner tonight in San Francisco? I know this lovely little cantina that makes the very best and freshest pasta."

"I'd love to," she said.

"Great," he said and he left to get ready for debarkation.

On the bridge, Tran was readying to take the SS Falcon out of hyper drive.

"We'll be arriving on the dark side of the moon, Captain, in 47 seconds," said Tran.

"All stop when we get there," said Stone.

"Yes, sir," said Tran.

And in a very short time after Stone had spoken to Tran, the SS Falcon slipped out of FTL and came to a full stop behind the dark side of the moon.

"Contact Sputnik," said Stone, "and let them know we have arrived. And let's just stay back here behind the moon and keep our wits about us. Remember, we're home late and Vitran had suggested we'd be fired upon if we came home late. I didn't believe him, but let's err on the side of caution."

"Aye, Captain," said Tran.

Ensign Tran tapped into his console to contact Space Station Sputnik. He waited several seconds, the smile on his face slowly disappearing. He tried again.

"They're not responding, Captain," Tran said.

Stone looked up, confused.

"Try again," he said.

"I've tried three times now, Captain," said Tran. "No response."

"Hail them on all frequencies," said Stone.

Tran tapped into his console again and waited. He did it two more times.

"I'm sorry sir," he said. "I am getting no response from them."

Stone stood up from his chair, and Tyrell Suggs stood up with him. They moved halfway across the bridge towards the main viewer.

"Okay, bring us up just over the ridge of the moon and let's see what's going on," said Stone. "Engage shadow cloaking and full shields as well."

Tran brought the SS Falcon up over the lip of the moon so they could get a better view of Earth. The Earth rose in front of them like a large bejeweled golf ball. Almost the whole of Earth was lit up by the sun. But the scene that greeted them was not what they expected. At this distance they could see bright sparks and splashes of light, lighting up like a halo around Earth.

"What on Earth!" exclaimed Suggs.

"Zoom in," said Stone.

Tran zoomed in on the main viewer and what they saw, frightened them. There were advanced spaceships of all kinds engaged in heated battle. On the surface of the Earth, explosions were dotting its face like rain drops on a puddle.

"Lieutenant Scot Free, what is going on there, I can't recognize any of those ships. Are you certain this is Earth?" asked Stone.

"I am quite certain, Captain," said Scot Free.

He tapped into his terminal as a stream of data brought up analysis of what they were seeing.

"It appears, Captain," said Scot Free, turning around to face him, "that in our enthusiasm at arriving home we failed to check the date."

"It should be 2898.288, correct?" said Stone.

"No sir," started Scot Free.

"Get on with it Lieutenant, what is going on here!" shouted Captain Stone.

"We entered through a wormhole that bent both space and time, Captain. The date is 3403.034.0343 to be precise."

There was stunned silence on the bridge of the Falcon for several seconds.

"You're saying we've arrived five hundred years in the future?" asked Jenks.

"That's a crude approximation, Commander," said Scot Free.

Jenks walked up to him and looked over his shoulder. He saw the date for himself.

"And the computer isn't wrong?" asked Suggs.

"No, sir, I have double checked and triple checked with the placement of known stars from our current coordinates. We have wound up far into the future. I didn't recognize the technology of any of those spaceships out there. They are vastly superior to anything I have or my builders have ever encountered. And now I know why," said Scot Free.

"Captain," said Suggs, "perhaps we should contact Star Ship Command and see what's going on?"

Stone nodded as he stroked his chin with his thumb and forefinger.

"Ensign, hail SSC on all channels, all known frequencies. Encrypted of course," said Stone.

"Hailing them, Captain," said Tran as he tapped into this console. "I have a response."

"Main viewer," said Stone.

An older woman in a uniform unrecognized by the crew of the SS Falcon appeared blurrily on the main viewer. The visual connection was not good, but the audio was clear.

"SS Falcon, I am Admiral Emmons, what are you doing here," she said.

"Admiral, I am Captain Jack Stone. Can you tell us what is going on? Is this really the 31st century?"

The image of the woman nodded.

"It is Captain. Our records show that you never made it back to Earth in the 29th century. You were assumed dead."

"Well, as you can see, we are very much alive. We managed to get back through a wormhole, but it bent space as well as time. Our crew is very tired and eager to debark. Can you give us instruction?" asked Stone.

The woman shook her head.

"Captain," said Admiral Emmons, "if you value your life and the life of your crew, you will leave immediately. For the last three years we have been involved in a battle to the death with the alien species VEA. They never gave us a name, they came quickly, quietly and attacked us, so we named them Very Evil Aliens or VEA. They don't take prisoners. Humanity has been decimated... lost almost... population."

"Admiral," said Stone, "we're losing your connection, can you repeat."

"Lost... ninety percent... leave... you will die..."

The last they saw of Admiral Emmons was of her turning around to watch as two aliens in black pointed at her and made their way towards her.

"Incoming message," said Tran.

"On screen," said Stone.

An image of the bridge of a small ship came onto the screen. A man wearing the same style of uniform as Admiral Emmons could be seen.

"Help, I'm under attack by VEA warships. Please engage," he said and then the connection was lost.

The ship darted in front of them, followed by another alien ship. These were small ships, probably didn't hold more than a handful of crew. They were about a tenth of the size of the SS Falcon.

"Jenks," said Stone, "fire pulson torpedoes on that alien ship."

"Don't you think that's a little overkill, Captain, look how small they are," said Jenks.

"Very well, fire pulsars," said Stone.

Jenks fired the pulsars and they made their mark. But nothing happened. They hit the alien ship and just disappeared. No damage.

"Perhaps pulson torpedoes as you suggested, Captain," said Jenks.

"And with haste," said Stone.

Jenks locked in a couple of pulson torpedoes and fired.

"I wonder how that pilot knew we were here," said Stone mostly to himself, though Suggs was within earshot. "We are, after all, under cloaking."

"Could be their technology, Captain," said Suggs.

The torpedoes made their mark and fizzled in little sparks. The alien ship was closing in on the star ship.

"Try again!" yelled Stone. "Give them all we've got."

Jenks locked in six pulson torpedoes and let them rip. Just as they were about to hit the alien ship, the alien ship fired on the star ship. A small white ball of light left the nose of the alien ship at incredible speed and made its mark on the star ship just a moment later. The star ship was incinerated in a fraction of a second. The pulson torpedoes seemed downright leisurely compared to the speed of the alien's ball of light. But they made their mark on the alien ship and, like the previous torpedoes they just fizzled on its shell.

"I can't believe it," said Stone. "Those torpedoes are amongst the most advanced and powerful weapons Space Fleet has produced. And nothing. Not even a scuff on his bumper."

"If I may, Captain," offered Scot Free. "We are, in this time period, nothing more than benign historic artifacts at best."

"Always looking on the bright side, hey Scot Free," said Jenks.

Scot Free smiled.

"Trying to call it as it is," Scot Free said. "Our best offense, Captain, in these circumstances is perhaps defense. Perhaps we should leave while we have a chance."

"Not on my watch," said Stone. "So long as we have pulson torpedoes to use, we'll use them in the protection of our home."

Jenks smiled.

"I'm with you Jack," he said.

"Listen," said Stone, "those of you who want to leave, you can leave now via escape pods. You have five minutes to make that decision and grab what personal items you'd like."

Stone made the same announcement over the ship's speaker system. Nobody on the bridge moved.

"What kind of a first officer would I be," said Suggs.

"Well, it doesn't appear that there is much of a home to go to," said Kelly. "Let's see if we can't go out with a bang."

"You have my vote," said Carvalho.

Stone looked at Scot Free. Scot Free looked back at him and raised his eyebrow.

"What, me?" said Scot Free. "I live to serve."

And he smiled wryly.

And so it was that the officers on board the SS Falcon decided to fight with 500 year old technology against an advanced alien race they had never before encountered.

"Jenks, how many torpedoes do we have left?" Stone asked.

"83," he said.

"Good," said Stone. "We're out gunned and we're out smarted by five hundred year old technology. I suggest we attack the mother ship, if there is one and if we can find it and access its soft belly. These small fighter ships give me reason to think that there is a mother ship, and she might not be that far away"

"Lieutenant Scot Free, see if you can't determine the best approach and best target for an attack, and see if there is a mother ship at all," said Stone.

Scot Free entered and read information from the computer. It took a few minutes, as the SS Falcon skulked out of the way back behind the dark side of the moon. No more alien or Earth based ships came around the dark side. All of the fighting was between the near side of the moon and Earth itself.

"Those of you who are still on board the SS Falcon, you have my gratitude and my respect. We will likely die out here on this black night. But we fight for the very existence of our home, of Earth. It has been my privilege to lead you all, these thirteen days," said Stone, both over the intercom and to the bridge crew now standing beside him.

"I have my best suggestion," said Scot Free.

"And it is?" asked Stone.

"A suicide mission, Captain. There is a mother ship and I have found it. The mother ship is tracking slowly behind Mars for protection, between Mars and the asteroid belt. She is not well protected though she has her own armament and shielding. By my calculations, it will take at least eighty torpedoes to make a tear in her shielding big enough for the SS Falcon to enter. And it will take the remaining torpedoes as well as the combined energy of our hyper and LUX drives to create a massive enough explosion to annihilate her. This hinges of course on making that tear with pinpoint accuracy right in her guts, where her drive is most vulnerable. I have ascertained that point."

"Why not just sit here and light up space as the alien ships come on by. Why not fight right where we are, surreptitiously?" asked Suggs.

"Because, Commander, you have seen how helpful our pulson torpedoes are in damaging the alien warships. The mother ship's shielding is not as robust and not as quick to change harmonics as the warships seem capable off. Additionally, it'll take a massive amount of torpedoes, as I just said, to create a tear big enough for the SS Falcon to enter. We couldn't possible keep up with a warship and manage to accurately pinpoint eighty torpedoes on target. Furthermore, we'll need to adjust the harmonics slightly for each third torpedo in order to create this tear we need."

"It seems like a sound plan to me, Captain," said Carvalho. "We'll likely need ten minutes to adjust the torpedo harmonics."

"Then you better get to it," said Stone.

"Already on it," said Carvalho. "I can access Engineering and Weapons schematics from the bridge, as well as Scot Free's harmonization schematics."

Carvalho headed over to the far side of the bridge where he started inputting codes and information into the computer.

"But how will disabling a mother ship from the far side of Mars help the battle raging here on Earth?" asked Suggs.

"I was getting to that Commander, and that is probably the most important aspect of this plan of attack," said Scot Free. "Firstly, this is the mother ship. In other words they don't have another one that I can detect within three light years. Secondly, and this is the key reason why we need to attack the mother ship and why we need to be successful. The mother ship is the source of their power. If we are successful at disabling the her, within minutes, all warships that are currently attacking Earth will lose ninety percent of their power. As warships, they'll practically become impotent."

"Have you calculated our chance of success with this approach?" asked Stone.

"I have, Captain, and I can say with great certainty that our likelihood of success, if we accurately pinpoint the torpedoes and create this tear that we need, will be 77 percent."

Stone nodded and gritted his teeth.

"I would have liked better odds for a suicide mission," said Stone.

"Captain," said Scot Free, "these are terrific odds. We have now twice entered wormholes that have brought us closer to home and each one only had a 73 percent chance of success. To use an old colloquial saying from Earth, I view this as practically a slam dunk."

"Scot Free," said Kelly, "you sound almost buoyant with optimism when in effect you are sending us all to our deaths. How can you be so cavalier about it?"

"Forgive me, Doctor," said Scot Free, "I do not mean to sound cavalier about this suicide mission. But it is the only choice I have been able to come up with that has the best chance of saving Earth, and your progeny. In fact, it is the only option we have of saving Earth and we don't have much time to decide."

Scot Free turned around and pointed to the main viewer.

"As you can see," he said, "Earth is being decimated as we sit here and chat about it. That blue jewel, your home, is practically in its death throes."

"And you are quite happy to give your life for our cause?" asked Suggs.

"I am Commander," said Scot Free, "my builders never programmed me with any fear or philosophy of death. And I have become fond of you. It would be an honor to stand with you shoulder to shoulder in our final fight. To stand shoulder to shoulder with all of you."

Scot Free looked around as he said this, his right arm cutting an arc with his palm facing upwards as he looked at each of them in turn.

Stone smiled.

"Well, Lieutenant," he said, "I believe I speak for all of us when I say that we have become quite fond of you too. You have turned out to be a great ally and loyal friend."

Scot Free nodded.

"And you are one hundred percent certain that there is no other choice available to us?" asked Stone.

"I am certain, Captain. I wish there were another option, I understand how you would rather not lose your lives."

"Okay then, team, we're off on a suicide mission. Those of you unwilling, may leave now," said Stone. "Carvalho are you ready?"

"Two more minutes," said Carvalho.

"Ensign, maximum LUX to Mars," said Stone.

"Aye, Captain," replied Tran.

Stone turned to Kelly and put his hand on her forearm.

"I'm sorry it turned out like this, but perhaps Earth will survive because of our sacrifice," said Stone.

Kelly looked at him. Her eyes were a little misty but she put on a brave face and confident smile.

"I'm not sorry," she said, "there isn't any home to go to if we don't do this. And there's nobody I'd rather be with under these circumstances."

Stone smiled at her and squeezed her shoulder.

"Lieutenant, have you locked in the coordinates for the torpedo barrage?" asked Stone.

"I have, Captain," said Scot Free. "As soon as we get within range, the volley will start on your mark."

"Good," said Stone. "Ensign, let's go."

And with that the SS Falcon took off at maximum LUX speed, just under the speed of light. The trip took them just under five minutes and they came to a crawl just beyond visual range of the mother ship.

"Captain," said Scot Free. "We'll be detected shortly I'm sure, even with shadow cloaking engaged. We must use the element of surprise to our advantage."

"Carvalho?" said Stone.

"Torpedoes are all ready," said Carvalho.

"Lieutenant Scot Free, you have helm control. When you're ready, get us in position," said Stone.

"Aye, Captain," said Scot Free.

The SS Falcon rose up behind the horizon of Mars and the mother ship, about one hundred times larger than they, loomed up ahead of them. They were at its rear, which is exactly where they wanted and needed to be. Three seconds later the ship filled practically the whole main viewer screen, looming as large as the Titanic seemed to be next to the life rafts.

"Now, Captain," said Scot Free. "We must fire now."

"Fire!" shouted Captain Jack Stone on Earth's life raft, the ancient SS Falcon.

Jenks tapped into the terminal and a stream of torpedoes shot out from the Falcon at the pace of seven or eight per second. After a second the first torpedoes started fizzling against the big mother ship. At first nothing seemed to happen. But then slowly, the way an eraser makes a small tear on a piece of paper over dozens of strokes, a small tear started opening up after a few seconds of the volley of torpedoes.

"It's working, Captain," said Scot Free.

And just as he spoke those words, a steady stream of laser like pulses were fired from the mother ship at the SS Falcon. They hit their mark and rocked the crew.

"Shields are down to 37 percent, Captain," said Commander Timothy Jenks. "We can't sustain much more of this."

"Carvalho," said Stone, "give Jenks every morsel of power you can spare. Hell, cut environmental controls to bare minimum."

"You bet, Jack," said Carvalho.

And the stream of lasers from the mother ship continued to thrash against the shields and outer hull of the SS Falcon.

"Shields are weakening!" yelled Jenks. "Down to 23 percent, Captain."

"We only need a few more seconds," said Stone. "Steady, steady."

And the last of the volley of torpedoes needed to open up a tear left the SS Falcon and exploded against the mother ship's hull. It had managed to rip through the shields.

"Give me the last of the torpedoes," said Scot Free, "and we'll be going in after."

"Fire!" yelled Stone.

Jenks fired the remaining three torpedoes and they exploded like fireworks against the battered mother ship's guts.

"This is going to work, Captain, here we go," said Scot Free, and you could almost hear the excitement in the tone of his voice.

"So this is how the world ends," said Stone, "with a bang."

Kelly squeezed his knee as the SS Falcon slammed through the tear and straight into the weakened and vulnerable guts of the mother ship. The last thing Stone saw was a magnificent white explosion that was incredibly warm.

"Captain," said the voice. "Captain Jack Stone?"

It sounded sincere and earnest. It was close by and friendly. Stone blinked his eyes and tried to open them, but the light was sharp and hot and blindingly white against his eyeballs. He blinked them again and again. Slowly, he started to focus and he saw a young woman dressed in pale blue looking down at him. She was smiling. She seemed human.

"Captain Jack Stone," she said. "You made it."

ABOUT SYLYNT STORME

Ever since I was a little kid I used to fly around my backyard pretending I was a Jedi Warrior or Federation Captain. When I say fly I mean run around pretending I was in a space ship.

Me and my friends used to take wooden rulers and paint and draw elaborate controls on them and these were our joysticks. We had X-wing fighters and USS star ships and we would spend hours exploring alien worlds and getting into dog fights. The good guys always won.

When I got a bit older I started to absorb everything I could about vampires, going through my own goth and vampire stage. I loved how cool they were and how they were sort of like super beings or demi-gods.

Not even werewolves could outfox vampires. These mysterious blood suckers were lurking around every dark corner of night, just waiting to pounce on unsuspecting victims.

And so now I write both science fiction and vampire horror stories because I still can't control my active imagination. I hope you enjoy my humble offerings. You can reach me at SylyntStorme@gmail.com.

Visit me at www.SylyntStorme.com to stay up to date on new stories as they come out.

OTHER BOOKS BY SYLYNT STORME

Sylynt Storme currently writes both science fiction and horror stories. The Star Sails series of which this book is a part is a space opera very much imbued in the Star Trek tradition.

This book you've finished reading is Star Sails: Four Pack Volume Two and contains the stories of the Star Sails series numbered 5, 6, 7 and 8. All Star Sails stories can be bought individually. You can also buy Star Sails stories numbered 1, 2, 3 and 4 as a four pack. Star Sails: Four Pack Volume One contains stories numbered 1, 2, 3 and 4.

Here are the complete series of Star Sails stories written to date. Please visit www.SylyntStorme.com for new stories as this is an ongoing series:

1. Dark Matter
2. Scot Free
3. Short Memory
4. False Gods
5. Tin Machines
6. Brother's Keeper
7. Worm Turns
8. Earth Rise

Additionally, Sylynt Storme writes horror stories, or more specifically, vampire stories under the series called The Misgivings of the Vampire Lucius Lafayette. Please visit www.SylyntStorme.com for more information on where to buy any of the collections or individual short stories for all e-readers. Additionally, the compilations are available in paper as well.